RAILS WEST

'Been waiting for you,' he replied. 'Take off that nightdress and come in here.' He opened the bed, his eyes narrowed as he saw her strip off. The next instant she was with him under the single cover and their naked bodies pressed together. He gathered her gently into his embrace, stroking her face, smoothing the hair from her temples while she pushed herself against his big, powerful frame. He drew his fingers along the side of her face and her neck, touching her shoulders lightly before permitting his gentle fingers to caress her breasts. She shivered involuntarily as he slipped one hand beneath her shoulders and enveloped her in his embrace. He kissed her gently, trying to contain his passion, but already he was throbbing with powerful male desire, and the soft warmth of her flesh further inflamed him.

Also by Bart Shane in this savage series of the real West

IRON RAILS

RAILS WEST

Bart Shane

A MOAT HALL BOOK
published by
Magread Limited

A Moat Hall Book
Published in 1980 by
Magread Limited
178–180 Wardour Street
London W1

© Bart Shane, 1980

Printed in Great Britain by
Hunt Barnard Printing Ltd., Aylesbury, Bucks.

ISBN 0 427 00437 3

Chapter One

The train was travelling through a long line of low hills south of Albuquerque and making hard work of the steeper grades. The passenger car jolted spasmodically, rattling in protest against the stresses of the curves and slopes, and the rhythmic sound of flanged wheels upon iron rails was never-ending, marking off the endless miles that stretched between the sun-tortured towns of New Mexico. Chet Manning, chief trouble-shooter for the South and West Railroad Company, sat facing the engine, lounging in a corner by a window, his brown eyes half-closed under his new grey stetson, which he had eased forward over his face. He was wearing a neat grey store suit, and his holstered Colt .45 was buckled around his waist. Spare bullets for the gun glinted in the loops of his cartridge belt. Heat had caused tiny beads of sweat to form upon his broad forehead. He breathed shallowly, and his head nodded in sympathy with the motion of the train.

But he was not asleep, as those around him supposed, and he was keenly aware of the sober-faced girl of about twenty-five facing him in a seat across the aisle. The fact that she was travelling alone made him glance at her from time to time from under the cover of his hat, his keen brown eyes mentally undressing her desirable body. She kept sighing heavily, gazing from the closed window at the hills and desolate scenery.

The sight of her reminded Manning of Netta Blaine, niece of his District Superintendent, Asa Blaine, who was based at Buffalo Junction, and his lips tightened as he fought down a pang of emotion. He stifled a sigh and shook his head, lifting his hat to peer from the window, but not really seeing the wilderness. Travelling south, they would soon be running into Gadson Flats, and after that was Buffalo Junction.

He was not looking forward to returning to duty. The wounds

on his big, raw-boned body from his last tough gunfight were healed, leaving only scars as grim reminders. He had killed Ben Yaro and ended a grave threat to S & W, but guessed that Western Pacific, their rivals, would still be determined to reach Apache Pass first – the only route through the Chamos Mountains and the gateway to Las Corros, the rapidly expanding town which would eventually become the railhead of the entire South-West. It was a glittering prize for the railroad company that won the desperate race to Apache Pass, and Western Pacific had no scruples about using every means available to them.

Manning looked at the girl again, feeling a twinge of desire uncoiling inside him, and knew that what he needed now was a good woman – any woman. He had spent long enough recuperating from his wounds.

His dark gaze swung to take in the rest of his fellow-passengers. Two men interested him: one, evidently a rancher, was medium-sized, dark-faced, wearing a Colt .45 on a sagging gunbelt. The other was dressed in black broadcloth and handled the cards with which they were playing like a professional gambler. They were using a flat travelling case, propped on their knees, as a table. The low murmur of their voices as they played mingled with the monotonous rhythm of the train as it continued southwards.

Manning returned his gaze to the girl. She wore a green hoopskirt which did not conceal her lithe figure, and there was a small white hat perched on her shining black hair. Her eyes were dark, her smooth skin tanned, and her teeth glinted whenever she parted her full red lips. He fought down a surge of desire and caught his breath, his wishful thinking about tumbling her in the baggage car almost too vivid to tolerate. She must have felt the intensity of his gaze for she looked up suddenly, turning from the window to return his stare, and Manning, caught unawares, smiled slowly in silent apology for his boldness.

'Can you tell me how much farther it is to Buffalo Junction, please?' she asked in a low tone.

'About another seven hours, miss. We've got Gadson Flats first.' He paused, wanting to strike up a conversation, but she looked so sad that he could not help wondering what had blighted her life. 'Are you getting off at Buffalo Junction?'

'Yes.' She looked away quickly, as if disturbed by his attention, and Manning stifled his next question and looked through the window at the wild scenery. He knew almost every yard of this terrain, and most of it held poignant memories for him.

A curse suddenly shattered the peacefulness and Manning looked up quickly. The two men playing cards were stiff as they faced one another, and the rancher, whose face Manning could see, was pale with anger.

'You're cheating, you four-flusher!' he rasped. 'I been watching you ever since we left San Blanca. Now I got you dead to rights!'

'Careful, mister,' the other replied smoothly. 'I don't take that kind of talk, even allowing for your anger.'

Manning got to his feet. The girl looked up at him with fear springing into her eyes. He moved easily, taking a long stride which put him beside the two men.

'What's the trouble?' he demanded sharply, and both men looked up at him.

'What's it to you?' demanded the gambler.

'I caught him cheating,' the rancher snapped. 'He's got at least two aces on him that ain't in the pack.'

The gambler made a quick movement towards a shoulder holster, causing the other to curse and reach for his .45. Manning palmed his sixgun smoothly and fast, and they both froze when they found themselves gazing at its steady black muzzle. The rancher was tense, his dark eyes burning with anger, but the menace of Manning's big .45 was too much for him and he took his hand off the butt of his holstered weapon. The gambler's hand was inside his coat, but he did not move. His smooth features were set in a bland expression which showed no emotion.

'What in hell are you horning in for?' demanded the rancher. 'I can take care of this sneaking cardsharp. I've handled his kind before.'

'There are other passengers on this train,' Manning replied, 'and I don't want to see any of them getting hurt by flying lead.' He waggled his gun slowly. 'Let me see you both pull your guns, but slowly, and lay them down where they won't hurt anyone.'

'You got no right,' complained the rancher.

'I've got all the right in the world. I'm Chet Manning, troubleshooter for this railroad. So sit still and I'll check out your claim that this *hombre* is cheating.'

'Chet Manning!' The anger faded from the rancher's voice and he gulped as he looked up. 'Are you *the* Chet Manning?'

'I wouldn't know about that. I'm the *only* Chet Manning, I reckon.'

'You put paid to Ben Yaro and his gang some weeks back!' the rancher persisted. 'And before that it was the Delmont gang. Are you *that* Chet Manning?'

'The same.' Manning smiled tightly when he saw the gambler remove his hand from inside his coat as if the butt of his concealed gun had suddenly grown hot. 'That's better,' he commented. 'Now let's get down to cases.'

'He's been cheating, and I didn't catch him at it until now,' the rancher accused. 'I suspected it almost from the start, but he's real smart. You'll find an ace, mebbe, up his right sleeve.'

'Take off your coat,' Manning ordered.

'Now see here!' the gambler said indignantly. 'If you're an employee of the Railroad then you'd better remember that I am a fare-paying passenger. I've got some rights.'

'Sure, and I'll see that you get everything you're entitled to.' Manning motioned with his gun. 'On your feet and take off that coat.'

The gambler arose slowly, his face shiny with sweat. The rancher dragged the snub-nosed pistol from the gambler's shoulder holster, throwing it down upon a seat, and Manning watched keenly as the gambler removed his black coat. Three cards fell to the floor from the sleeves and the rancher pounced on them, cursing angrily. He turned them up, revealing three aces, and swung on the gambler while reaching for his holstered gun.

'You dirty skunk! I'm down two hundred dollars to you!'

'You don't need that gun, mister,' Manning rapped, and the rancher halted his movement. 'Pay him back.' Manning eyed the gambler. 'There's a law against gamblers cheating on the railroad.'

The gambler produced a wallet and extracted a sheaf of bills. The rancher snatched the money and peeled off his losses, then flung the remainder back in the gambler's face.

'Are you satisfied?' Manning demanded, and the rancher

nodded reluctantly. 'Good. At your age you should know better than to play cards with a stranger on the train.' He looked at the gambler. 'That your case?'

'Yeah!' There was a trace of insolence in the man's voice. 'What you planning to do?'

'Pick it up and make your way to the baggage car.' Manning stepped back to give him room. They left the car and went to the rear of the train. The conductor was in the baggage car, and he frowned at the sight of them, but recognised Manning. 'Open that door, Silas,' Manning ordered, and the conductor obeyed, to reveal the countryside flashing by.

'What you got here, Chet?' the conductor demanded.

'Gambler.' Manning did not take his eyes off the man. 'Okay,' he snapped. 'Throw out your case, then jump after it.'

'What the hell!' The gambler shook his head resolutely. 'I got my ticket to Buffalo Junction.'

'You're getting off now, the easy way or the hard way.' There was a grim note in Manning's voice as he holstered his gun. 'If I catch you on any Company train in this area after today it will be more than a big jump for you. Now get going or I'll throw you off head-first.'

The gambler moistened his lips. 'I got two hundred dollars left,' he offered. 'It's yours for a ride into Buffalo Junction.'

Manning seized him by the shoulder and spun him to face the doorway. The landscape flashed by even faster as they hit a downgrade. The gambler yelled and tried to clutch at Manning, but he was propelled through the doorway, and Manning's last glimpse of him was a whirling tangle of limbs as the man fell to the hard ground beside the track.

'I hope he didn't break a leg,' the conductor remarked. 'It's a long way he's got to walk.'

Manning smiled tightly, removing his jacket because he was sweating, and he carried it, his shirt sleeves rolled up past his thick elbows, as he went back to his seat in the coach. There was a babble of excitement amongst the other passengers, but it cut off as he appeared. He resumed his seat in a significant silence, then the man who had been cheated called out.

'Thanks, Manning. This is one railroad a man can ride and count on being taken care of.'

Manning made no reply. He was aware that the girl was looking at him now, and let his gaze shift from her trim ankles

9

to her face. This time, as their gazes met, she smiled hesitantly.

'I overheard what was said.' Her voice was little more than a whisper. 'So you're Chet Manning! You must know my father.'

Manning frowned, wondering what was coming next. 'Who's your father?' he demanded gently.

'Ike Mozee. He was construction camp boss on the new track they're putting in until he was shot in the big raid.'

'Ike Mozee!' Manning could not prevent surprise sounding in his voice. 'Sure I know him, and very well! I blame myself for that raid he was wounded in. But I heard that he's on his feet again. I didn't know he had a daughter. He never talked about you.'

'I don't really know him myself. My mother left him years ago. She is dead now. When I heard about him getting shot in that raid I decided to come and visit him.'

'I'm glad to know you, Miss Mozee. Me and your pa are very good friends. I accidentally shot him once, and he knocked out one of my teeth on another occasion. When the chips are down there ain't a braver man than your pa.' He paused, and felt a trickle of emotion inside. 'I'm going back to Buffalo Junction for the first time since that last showdown. I got shot up some, but I'm all healed now and ready to get back into harness. I'll be happy to see you get to Buffalo Junction safely.'

'Thank you.' She smiled and came to join him, and he removed his hat as she sat down opposite. He saw her eyes flicker to his left forearm, and looked down at the long knife scar which marred his brown flesh from elbow to wrist.

'I'll roll down my sleeve if it bothers you,' he offered.

'No. That's all right.' She could not repress a shudder. 'It must have been a terrible fight, Mr Manning.'

'A souvenir from one of the enemies of the Railroad Company. I get quite a lot of scars.' He smiled easily.

'I read an account of the Yaro business,' she replied, her face turning pale. 'It was awful! How can you spend your life facing up to these risks every day?'

'I'm a railroader!' There was pride in his voice. 'I can't say more than that. Like my pa and yours, I live and breathe railroad.'

'It was the railroad which caused mother to leave my father,' she commented. 'The railroad is a harsh mistress.'

10

Manning nodded slowly. 'I agree with you. What's your given name?'

'Rosa.'

'I'm glad to know you, Rosa. I expect your father will get the shock of his life when he sees you, if he doesn't know you're coming. If I know him, he's itching to get back to work at the construction camp. I'll bet the doc couldn't keep him in bed despite the wound he got. The only thing he worries about is his schedule.'

'Is it very primitive living out here?'

'It is in the wilds, but you'll find Buffalo Junction quiet. It's the railroad's area town and we keep it under control.'

The hours seemed to flit by, Manning discovered, and he enjoyed the girl's company. They chatted until the train reached Buffalo Junction in the early evening, and he felt a pang of disappointment because the trip had come to an end. He collected Rosa's baggage, helped her off the train and, before he could set down the bags, Asa Blaine was at his back, his strident voice booming around the depot.

'Glad to see you back, Chet!' Blaine was medium-sized, chunky and powerful, with a broad, weathered face and a greying spade beard adorning his chin. 'You're looking fit!' His hard gaze searched Manning intently, looking beneath the exterior, and his strong face was creased with a beaming smile.

'I'm good as new, Asa,' Manning replied, shaking hands. 'How's business? I figure I've been away too long.'

'There's a lot I got to tell you but that can wait until we get into my office.' Blaine fell silent, becoming aware of the girl at Manning's side.

'Rosa, this is my boss, Asa Blaine, the District Superintendent,' Manning introduced. 'Asa, this is Rosa Mozee, Ike's daughter. I met her on the train.'

Blaine's heavy jaw dropped for a moment, and his beard waggled. Then he made an effort to recover from his surprise.

'Well I'll be hornswoggled!' he gasped. 'I'm danged if you ain't the image of your ma when she was your age. Heck, the last time I set eyes on you, young woman, you weren't no more than a little shaver who could hardly stand, let alone walk. Must be all of twenty years ago!'

'That's right, Mr Blaine,' she replied, smiling, her eyes glinting. 'I've heard mother talk about you many times! You've been a legend around the railroad for years.'

'How is your ma?'

'She died some time ago.' Her expression tightened.

'I'm real sorry to hear that. She was a handsome woman. I allus figured that Ike made a big mistake when he let your ma go and kept the railroad.'

'Thank you.' Rosa smiled.

'It was a bad thing your pa taking a slug like he did, but he was brave. We lost a lot of men in that raid, and Ike was one of the lucky ones. He raised the alarm that morning and saved a lot of lives. He's already back out there at the end of the track, worrying about his schedules and deadlines. But he ain't real fit yet. It was touch and go at the time. But he's as tough as those iron rails they're laying. The only thing that's gonna shake him is seeing you, Rosa.'

'I figure we'd better get her settled in at the hotel, huh?' Manning suggested.

'Not likely!' Asa shook his greying head. 'Aunt Polly knew Rosa's ma, and we'll put her up at our place. She'll be company for Netta. I don't know what's come over that gal lately. She's been moping around like a sick calf with no mother.'

'I'll take her over to the house and introduce her,' Manning said. 'How's Aunt Polly taking it about Willard?'

'He died a hero and we can't ask for more than that,' Asa retorted, shaking his head. 'She don't say much about it, but she's been hit real hard, Chet. I guess you coming back will put new life into her.'

'I can sure do with some of her cooking. But what about the situation, Asa? Any problems while I've been away? Have Western Pacific pulled in their horns since the Yaro trouble?'

'Come on back to my office when you get Rosa settled in at the house,' Asa replied. 'There is some business for you to handle, so if you are really fit again then be ready to get down to work immediately.'

'I'll be right with you.' Manning picked up Rosa's baggage and escorted the girl from the station.

They crossed the street to the Blaine house opposite, and Manning felt a surge of anticipation as they entered. He could hardly wait to get his hands upon Netta again, and thought of how the girl had saved his life down by the creek when Yaro's wife, Glory Harpe, working under cover, had trapped him for

12

two gunmen to finish off. He had made love to Netta in the bushes after the attack, and before he had been able to repeat the pleasure the showdown had exploded and he was wounded in the resultant shoot-out. But now he was as good as new, and he hoped Netta's moping around was on account of his absence.

Aunt Polly, a small, bird-like woman with a weathered face and deep, unfathomable eyes, peered out of the kitchen when she heard the front door open, and let out a screech of delight when she recognised Manning. She dropped a pan and came running to him, exclaiming in delight, throwing her arms around his neck, and he hugged her and swung her feet off the floor, kissing her wrinkled forehead before setting her down again.

'It's good to see you, Aunt Polly,' he said. 'How you coping now all the shooting and the shouting has died down?'

'It's wonderful to see you, Chet,' she replied. 'I'm glad you are back. The place has been dead without you around. Are you sure you're quite better now?'

'You know me.' He chuckled. 'You can't keep a good man down.' He turned to look at Rosa, who was watching them closely. 'This is Asa's wife, Polly. Aunt Polly, here's someone you have met before. Can you guess who she is?'

Aunt Polly put her head on one side and peered into the girl's face, shaking her head slowly when she failed to come up with an answer.

'The face is familiar, but I can't place it,' she admitted.

'The name is Rosa Mozee,' Manning said.

'Ike's daughter? Lands sakes, child! I nursed you on my knee many times when you was a babe in arms.'

Manning stepped back and watched the two women greeting each other. He could hear a sound in the parlour, and went to the door, peering into the room to see Netta laying the table for supper. The girl was tall, with blonde hair and blue eyes, and she worked uneasily, as if her mind was not upon her work. He let his gaze rove over her figure, recalling that morning in the bushes by the creek. A sigh gusted from him and he drew a sharp breath.

'Guess who's back!' he called.

'Chet!' She gazed at him as if he were a ghost, then came towards him, reaching out for him. 'I've been counting the days to your return. Why didn't you let us know you were coming?'

'In case something held me up and you got disappointed,' he replied, hugging her, feeling her soft, warm body against his own tough, scarred figure. 'But come on out here and meet someone who will be a friend to you. I guess you could do with some company around here, huh?'

'You're all I need,' she said in an undertone. Her blue eyes gleamed as she gazed at him. 'I want you,' she went on shamelessly. 'I don't care who knows it. After what's happened between us I'd like to tell the whole world.'

'Take it easy,' he said harshly. 'Don't talk like that. You know we can't let Asa know what happened, or what's going on between us.'

She sighed, and he pushed open the door and led her out to where Aunt Polly and Rosa were standing.

'I'll be back for supper,' he said. 'But right now I got to talk to Asa. He figures there's some work for me to do. Nothing like coming back and getting straight into it, huh?' He let his gaze go to Rosa. 'We'll send you out to end of track as soon as we can so you can see your pa. I'll probably be riding out that way myself tomorrow. See you later.'

He left the house and the woman-talk and went back across the street to the depot. Asa was waiting for him, standing in the doorway of his office, and Manning felt a chill sensation in the pit of his stomach as he entered, for it was in this office that Willard Blaine, Asa's son, had been killed.

'I'm real glad you're back, Chet,' Asa said without preamble, sitting down behind his desk and motioning Manning to a seat. 'I'm glad to say that Western Pacific have been forced to go easy on the dirty work. They got a lot of bad publicity after you finished off Yaro and his bunch, although nothing can be proved against them. The race for Apache Pass is still on and the situation remains the same. The first one to lay track in the Pass will get the franchise to open up the whole South-West. That's gonna be S & W, although Western Pacific have other ideas on that. But there is some trouble for you. It's been waiting for you to get back, you might say, and I figure you've got to handle it before you can settle down to any serious rail-road work.'

14

Manning frowned as he sat down and gazed into the older man's face.

'Trouble?' he demanded. 'Did I leave any loose ends from the Yaro business?'

'It stems from that.' Asa leaned forward in his seat. 'That saloon gal, Glory Harpe. You knew she was really Ben Yaro's wife, didn't you?'

'I found that out just before the showdown.' Manning nodded, his mind flitting back over past events. 'She was at the ranch when all the shooting started, but you let her go while I was on my back with that shoulder wound.'

'I didn't know she was Yaro's wife then. I thought she was just a saloon gal hanging around that robber's roost. I let her go when she promised to leave the district for good. Well we only took two prisoners from the Yaro gang – Trig Forbes, an out and out hardcase, and Grat Trimble, who ran the freight line here in Buffalo Junction and had branch offices in Gadson Flats and other places. It came out when Trimble was arrested that he was working under cover for Yaro, passing on information and the like.'

'So?' Manning interposed. 'Get to the point, Asa.'

'Last week someone went into the law office, smacked Hank Chilvers over the head with a gun barrel and busted those two outlaws out of the jail. There was a note left, Chet, written by Glory Harpe. She is burning up with hatred because you killed Yaro. She's sworn to see you dead!'

'Is that a fact?' Manning shook his head, unimpressed by the news. 'Has she been seen around with Forbes and Trimble since she busted them loose?'

'No, and that's worrying me. It could be that they're laying low until you get back. So watch your step, huh? You're gonna have to take things easy for a spell. You can't be fully fit yet. Jake Mullin has been doing a good job as your stand-in while you've been out of action. So I figure you better handle this unfinished business before you take over your regular job again. You don't want Forbes and Trimble getting behind you one dark night when you're least expecting it.'

'Yeah!' Manning breathed heavily for a moment, his strong face showing frustration. 'But I'm not afraid of that trio. I'm more interested in making sure we get to Apache Pass ahead of Western Pacific.'

'So am I!' Asa spoke harshly. 'But you can't get away from the fact that Glory Harpe hates your guts, Chet, and a woman like that is worse than any two hardcases. You're gonna have to do something about her.'

'Well I plan to look around the entire district before I start troubleshooting again, and I may run across them. I'll take care of them if I do.'

'I know you can take care of yourself, Chet, but those three hate the railroad almost as much as they hate you, and if they put their heads together and decide to get tough we could have a lot of trouble on our hands. It could be out of all proportion to their ability. Just three of them out there to hit us! We'd never find them. It was hard enough looking for Yaro and thirty men.'

'I know what you mean!' Manning shook his head. 'What do you want me to do, Asa?'

'I've got three good men out watching for Glory and her two hardcases. There's been no trouble along the railroad that we can't account for, so it's fairly obvious that they're laying low until you come back.'

'And here I am!' Manning drew a sharp breath as he considered. He had been dreading this minute from the time he had begun to recover from his wound. Something had happened to his mind because of that last shoot-out. He could not assess it, but did not think his nerve had gone. All he knew was that there was no pleasure in his job now, and he was not looking forward to the moment when he would have to draw his gun in defence of the railroad.

But he was the chief troubleshooter for S & W and the job was more than a mere name. It entailed carrying weapons and being prepared to use them in situations where a split-second reaction could mean the difference between life and death. It meant that he had to go out each morning and set himself up as a target, to try and get to grips with the ruthless, remorseless men who figured the railroad fair game for all known forms of trickery, robbery and murder. He had to be ready to lay down his life for any fare-paying passenger, and he was at the beck and call of all employees who needed help in complying with company rules.

He suddenly felt that he was no longer equal to the job. Western Pacific, their business enemies, would not give up

16

their murderous attempt to prevent S & W being first to Apache Pass, but Manning knew he had to keep his fear to himself, for if Asa became aware of this uncharacteristic anxiety he would find a replacement, and Manning realised that his problems might disappear the instant he saw action again. If it didn't he might be dead, then it wouldn't matter anyway!

Chapter Two

Three pairs of cold, intent eyes watched the train as Chet Manning kicked off the gambler. They saw the man hit the ground hard, rolling over and over before lying still, and waited until he recovered from the fall and began to sit up to take note of his surroundings. The trio were sitting their mounts on a near-by ridge, slump-shouldered in the hot sunlight. Grains of sand stung their faces. The train seemed to be disappearing into a blur of dust and heat haze, shimmering as it passed out of sight, the rumble of its passing echoing and re-echoing across the silent wilderness. One of the three was a woman dressed in red check shirt and faded blue Levis. Her face was set in harsh lines, dust-covered, her lips pinched, blue eyes narrowed and brooding. A gunbelt encircled her slim waist, containing a .38 revolver, and a dusty black, low-crowned stetson sat atop her blonde hair.

The two men were equally dusty and trail-weary. One was in his fifties, a tall, lean, scowling man with an habitual sneer on his twisted lips. His stained clothes bespoke rough living, but the gun on his right hip was dust-free. The other man was younger, around thirty-five, massively built with wide shoulders and powerful arms. His face was fleshy, set in hard lines, and his mouth was tight-lipped. His pale eyes, crinkled against the glare of the sun, were blue with white flecks in them, and they blazed with fanatical emotion. He stared after the train like a mountain cat scenting prey. Two crossed cartridge belts encircled his waist, and black butts flared from open holsters, each notched in mute testimony to the number of men killed by the weapons.

'What do you make of that, Glory?' the older man demanded. 'That feller was kicked off the train. He didn't jump!'

'It ain't none of our business, Trimble,' Trig Forbes said

18

in a clipped tone. 'We got enough on our plates without sticking our noses into other folks' business.'

'Trig, that ain't the attitude to take and you know it,' Glory Harpe countered. 'We've been watching the railroad for Chet Manning's return, so ride down there and pick up that *hombre*. Get him up here. I need to talk to him.'

Forbes shook his head in exasperation and kicked his mount forward over the ridge, raising dust as he rode down towards the track where the gambler was slowly getting to his feet and staring after the train. Grat Trimble watched until Forbes was out of earshot then looked at the woman with a calculating expression in his hard eyes.

'Glory, when you busted us out of jail I reckoned we could work together with no trouble. But with Forbes around I guess you've lost my interest. He ain't worried none about Chet Manning. It don't matter to him that all his pards got wiped out by Manning. But me and you are different. We got personal reasons for wanting that troubleshooter dead. He killed Ben and left me down in that disused well where the gold was hidden. I reckon we can forget that fool notion of making the railroad pay for what happened to the Yaro gang. Let's beef Manning and get the hell out of here. We're gonna have nothing but trouble with Forbes. You know he ain't quite right in the head. Your husband was the only man could keep him in check, and now Ben is dead Forbes is likely to go off the rails completely with no one holding the reins. He's figuring on gathering a new gang and running it himself. I don't want nothing to do with that. I ain't an outlaw! I was running that freight line at a profit while passing on information to Ben.'

'You're a fool, Grat, if you think nothing has changed. They picked you up during the showdown, and there's no chance you can go back to your old way of life. They know you for what you are. We are all outlaws now, and you would most likely hang with the rest of us for your part in all the trouble. Remember all those railroaders who were killed at the end of track? Nobody even remotely connected with that business is gonna live to talk about it. I busted you and Trig out of jail because I need you and we have the same aims in life.'

She fell silent, narrowing her pale eyes against the white glare of the sun and watching Forbes's progress towards the track. Her expression was ferocious, the veins in her smooth throat standing out, her nostrils flared like those of a nervous horse. Trimble watched her, fascinated by her hatred, for it matched his own. But he said nothing. He was afraid of Trig Forbes. He didn't trust the outlaw. Forbes was interested only in hitting the railroad for more money and, after what had happened to the rest of Yaro's gang, Trimble knew that any such attempt could only have the same fatal results.

'I got money in the bank in Buffalo Junction and Gadson Flats,' he said. 'It would be enough to live on until we nailed Manning.'

'But you can't get hold of that money! You're an escaped prisoner, a fugitive from the law, and the bank wouldn't hand over that dough even though it is yours. We need money, Grat, and Trig is the only man we know who can help us get some quickly. When Manning is dead we can split up, but until then we've got to stick together for survival.'

'I could get my dough,' he said harshly. 'I had a name for being honest. When your husband sent me in to watch points I put down roots and became honest. I got a taste for that kind of life. It was hard luck I had to be at Ryker's ranch when Manning came for the showdown. But for that I wouldn't have been caught. I'll bet if I saw Howard Belling in Gadson Flats he'd pay me out. We were good friends.'

'You can't trust anyone now!' she insisted. 'Not until Manning is dead. I've got no one in the world. Manning did this to me. I'm as good as dead because I'm alone. But I'll get even for it. I'll see Manning lifeless if it's the last thing I do, and I want to watch him die. I want to see him going down and dying slowly so I can confront him and tell him why he's dying. I want to see the agony in him and the life fading out of his eyes.'

Trimble's dark eyes glittered as he listened, and his hands clenched upon his reins. A crooked half-smile touched his tight-lipped mouth and he nodded slowly.

'By hell! I want that too, Glory! I'd give every cent of my dough in the banks just for the pleasure of watching Manning kick out his life in the dust. We've got to get even. It's all we have to live for.'

'That's what I keep telling you.' Glory spoke calmly. 'So we've got to work together, Grat.'

'But not with Forbes and that gang he wants to set up. We'll get ourselves mixed up with another crooked bunch and never get clear of them. They won't be interested in what we want to do. They'll start hitting the railroad again and stirring up all those troubleshooters. We can't afford that. We need to drop on to Chet Manning quietly, when he's least expecting trouble. If we can get him alone then we can nail him. With a gang around us we'd only be bringing attention to ourselves and making the job more difficult.'

Glory made no reply. Her teeth clenched as she recalled the recent past. Chet Manning had made love to her and she could not forget it although Yaro had set her up for Manning in order to lure him into a gun trap. But it hadn't worked, and when Manning wiped out her husband the shock had almost unhinged her mind. It did not matter to her that Manning had fought fairly in the showdown. Her husband was dead and Western Pacific were in trouble with their deadlines. S & W were on the move again towards Apache Pass despite the efforts of her dead husband.

Trig Forbes reined up in front of the motionless gambler, noting the black broadcloth suit and smooth appearance, and immediately tagged this man for what he was. His lip curled and he fought down the impulse to pull one of his guns and blast him to kingdom come. Instead he smiled, his fleshy face creasing into ugly lines.

'You in some kind of trouble?' he demanded hoarsely.

The gambler nodded slowly, taking in Forbes's rough appearance and not liking what he saw.

'You got throwed off that train,' Forbes continued. 'What for?'

'Some feller I was playing cards with figured I was cheating! It was my hard luck there was a railroad troubleshooter aboard, and he kicked me off.'

'Troubleshooter?' Forbes pinched his lips. 'Who was it? You got any idea?'

'Sure. He told me his name. Chet Manning! He pulled his gun on me slicker than a snake's tongue. I didn't try to argue with him, and he couldn't be bought. I offered him a couple of hundred bucks to let me finish the trip to Buffalo Junction but he grinned as he tossed me off the train.'

'You got two hundred bucks on you?' Forbes's pale eyes

21

glinted and a grin of anticipation touched his thick-lipped mouth. He reached instinctively for his right-hand sixgun, drawing the long-barrelled weapon and cocking it, the three clicks sounding ominous in the silence.

'You can have the dough!' the gambler croaked, his face turning pale. 'Hell, I sure got a run of bad luck this trip. Take my stake. It's in my inside pocket.'

'You got a gun in that shoulder holster?' Forbes queried, stepping down out of his saddle.

'No. It was took off me.'

'Well, get your hands up and I'll check you over. Never did like gamblers. They figure the odds too good for my liking. You're a snake breed, mister. Hoist 'em before I let daylight through you.'

The gambler thrust his hands high and stood very still, scarcely daring to breathe. He did not even blink as Forbes relieved him of his billfold and then the rest of his belongings. A gold watch disappeared into Forbes's pocket, then a diamond stick-pin and gold cuff links.

'That cleans me out, mister,' the gambler said softly.

'Open up your case and we'll see what's in it. I never knew a gambler yet who didn't split his stake in case he ran into trouble.'

The gambler nodded slowly and dropped to one knee, taking his time opening the flat case, and Forbes stood behind him, big sixgun levelled and steady. The gambler finally opened the case and flipped back the lid, snatching up a .38 Remington lying on top of his spare suit and swinging to bring the outlaw under its muzzle. But there was a wide grin of contempt on Forbes's heavy face and he thumbed off a shot that tore through the gambler's back, the impact tossing him across the case. The echoes blasted through the silence, across the barren horizon.

'I had you figured dead to rights, you smooth polecat!' Forbes sneered, holstering his gun and bending over the dead man. He thrust the body aside and went through the contents of the case, picking up another billfold which was thick with paper money. He grinned as he thrust the money into his pocket, and when he had checked that there was nothing else of value he swung into his saddle and rode back to the ridge.

Glory and Trimble were waiting impatiently for him, and

Trimble was taut with suppressed emotion. He didn't like Forbes's eager expression. The man was a cold-blooded killer, and it might not take much to turn him against those he now regarded as his friends. He could bite any friendly hand that was extended towards him.

'Why did you shoot him?' Glory demanded. 'Who was he and why did they kick him off the train?'

'Gambler!' Forbes spoke laconically, then grinned. 'He tried for a gun he was carrying in the case. I cleaned him out. He was carrying about five hundred bucks.' He paused and studied Trimble's harsh expression, and a shivering impulse flared inside him. He didn't like Trimble, and was tempted to put a slug through the snivelling crook who figured he was a cut above the usual run of outlaws. But he stayed his hand. Trimble might be useful later. He switched his gaze to Glory, his eyes glittering as he studied her trim figure, and his grin widened, his thoughts roving. They had been in her bed at the ranch when Manning arrived for the showdown. But since Yaro died and she had busted him out of jail she had not permitted him to touch her, and he was lusting for a woman. He controlled his feelings and drew a sharp breath. 'Got some news from that *hombre* before he cashed in his chips. You know who happened to be on that train when he started cheating?'

'Tell me!' Glory snapped, her face turning pale as she guessed whose name was coming.

'Chet Manning. All healed up from his wounds and back to take up his job. That's what you've been waiting for, huh?' He grinned at the sight of the naked fury which flared in her expression.

Glory's eyes blazed and she clenched her hands, sending a string of unladylike curses through the brooding silence. Trimble shifted uneasily in his saddle, tightening his slitted trap of a mouth as he hoped that soon this nightmare existence with a kill-crazy woman and a cold-blooded killer would be over. But he needed them right now! He could not survive by himself in this harsh wilderness and he could not ride into any town without fear of arrest. But now Manning was back they could begin to lay their plans, and when Manning was dead he would be able to depart. But until then he had to stick with this unsavoury pair.

'What are we gonna do now?' he demanded hoarsely, pulling

his hat lower over his eyes. The sun burned down, lying across their shoulders like a physical burden.

'You know what we're gonna do!' Glory retorted. 'We'll ride south to Buffalo Junction. In the morning we can cut down Manning before he gets back to troubleshooting. I don't want him to live a moment longer than necessary. He should be in his grave right now, and would be if I'd known where they sent him to recover.'

'Hold your hosses,' Forbes cut in. 'How'd you reckon me and Trimble are gonna nail Manning? You figure we'll mebbe ride into town, look him up and start the shooting?' He shook his head, grinning wryly. 'You should know better than that! Yaro tried more than once to get Manning in a gun trap. You took part in one yourself with Creed and Penner, two of our fastest guns, and failed to get him. So I ain't likely to try the same thing, especially with a creep like Trimble siding me. Even in the showdown, Manning nailed four men then took on Yaro and Brannigan together and got them. He's a *hombre* who is hard to kill. Some men have that kind of luck! He's one of them. I ain't risking my neck in an open attempt to blast him. This has got to be worked out carefully. We got to make plans.'

'I don't figure it that way,' Trimble said obstinately. 'Chet Manning might be fast and accurate with a gun, but he can't do a blame thing about a bullet in the back. I'll ride into Buffalo Junction and lay for him. I'll cut him down when he ain't expecting it.'

'No!' Glory's voice was high-pitched and grated in the silence. 'I don't want him dead that way. I want to be standing in front of him, looking in his face when he goes down. He's got to know who is killing him and why.'

'Hell, he can only die!' Trimble protested. 'I'll be satisfied just to see him lifeless.'

'That's not good enough for me!' There was a fierce note in Glory's voice. 'If you don't figure to play it my way, Trimble, then light out of here and get lost. I'll kill Manning myself. All I need is some help to take him alive. Then you can leave me alone with him.'

Forbes drew a sharp breath, fascinated by Glory's hatred. But he had no intention of sticking with this pair, although he fancied that they might come in useful in the near future. Glory had busted him out of jail but he did not appreciate the fact. All he needed her for was sex, and he was getting tired of being rejected when they had already been lovers. He was again tempted to pull his gun and down Trimble. He didn't like the man's constant bellyaching about the situation. Trimble was a two-bit crook like the rest of them, but figured he was better than most, and he was riding for a fall although he didn't know it yet.

'Listen to me,' he said thickly, and a pulse beat in his throat as he watched Glory easing herself in the saddle. He wanted her badly and could feel the heat rising inside him like a wave. 'You both wanta see Manning dead, huh?'

'You know that's right,' Glory retorted.

'Okay.' Forbes grinned. The vengeful lines around his mouth deepened a little. He was a born killer, filled with strange lusts, and a flame of twisted emotion burned in his pale eyes. 'But I figure you could have more fun at his expense while he's still alive, before you finish him off. He's the chief troubleshooter of the S & W. So let's give him some more trouble. If we handle it right he won't get near to nailing us, and when we've run him ragged and broken him you can kill him. What do you say to that, Glory? And you know Yaro's contact with Western Pacific. They're still ready to pay good money for S & W to be stopped.'

'No deal,' Trimble said without hesitation. 'We know Yaro was smarter than all of us put together, and look what happened to him. I don't figure the three of us can handle Manning better than Yaro and the gang, and they wasn't near good enough.'

'I should have been the boss of the gang!' Forbes replied, an angry glitter coming into his blue eyes. 'I told Ben several times that he was playing it all wrong but he wouldn't listen to me. I could have done it better.' He snickered. 'I couldn't have handled it worse, huh?'

Glory nodded slowly, her eyes filled with bright hatred. 'What's on your mind, Trig?' she invited. 'You got something ticking over, I can tell.'

He grinned, nodding excitedly. 'Listen. A week before Ben was killed and the rest of the gang wiped out we met up with the survivors of Squint Delmont's gang. They wanted to join us but Ben wouldn't have them. I figure they would welcome the chance of revenge against Manning, and I got an idea where they are hiding out. I reckon to ride over and ask them to throw in with us. We've got to make a living while we're waiting to take Manning, and two men and a woman ain't enough to grab dough from the railroad. We'd probably have to settle for robbing stage coaches, and there ain't so many of them now the railroad is running through the country.'

'I don't want to get mixed up with no bunch of crooks,' Trimble said, shaking his head firmly. 'I ain't a crooked man at heart. You can count me out of the kind of deal you're fixing. I want no part of it. All I want is to see Manning dead.'

'You're a fool, Trimble,' Forbes retorted. 'You got plenty of money in the bank in Buffalo Junction and in Gadson Flats, but you can't touch a red cent of it. Manning did that to you. It's up to you to get your own back. Throw in with us and you'll get everything you want.'

'Think it over, Grat,' Glory suggested. 'If we kill Manning quick we'll miss the pleasure of gloating over his downfall. I figure Trig has a good idea. If it takes a few weeks to work his plan it might be worth it, and we can down Manning any time we want. I'm for it. S & W took away your living. Let's get something back before we end it for Manning, and if we do a good job then Western Pacific will still pay what they promised the gang.'

Trimble looked at the woman, and shivered as he took in her utterly merciless expression. He was aware that Forbes was studying him intently, and was afraid that the outlaw would shoot him down in cold blood if he refused to fall in with their wishes. He could always drop out of it one dark night. He nodded slowly, forcing a grin.

'Okay,' he said, using just the right amount of unwillingness in his voice. 'I don't have anything else to lose. I'll go along with it.'

'I agree,' Glory said, 'but only on the understanding that when I want Manning, you and the others will help take him alive for me, Trig.'

'That's a deal I'll be eager to keep,' Forbes said without hesitation. 'Now you ride on over the ridge, Trimble, and wait for Glory. I got a few things to talk over with her, and when I ride off to locate those three men from Delmont's gang you and Glory go back to the hideout and wait for me. When I get back we'll be in business again.'

Trimble stared at Forbes for a moment, then shrugged his thin shoulders and gigged his mount over the crest and began to ride down the reverse slope. Glory looked at Forbes as he rode in beside her, and when he grasped her reins she compressed her lips.

'Me and you have got some business to settle before I ride off,' he said. 'Since Ben's been dead we ain't got together none, and I'm burning up for you, Glory. Get out of your saddle and make yourself ready for me. I aim to pleasure you before I go.'

'Quit that, Trig. I told you I don't want nothing more to do with you in that way.'

'That's too bad. I need a woman and you're the only one around. Either you do like I want or I ride off now and don't come back. I can't see you and Trimble getting Manning without my help. If you want me to help you then you got to help me.'

'You can get a woman anywhere, soon as you reach a town,' she countered firmly. 'I told you before that you and me have had it as far as that goes. It's all washed up between us and I ain't going back on my word. If you figure to blackmail me into doing what you want then you got another think coming, Trig. I ain't playing along.'

'You used to like what we got up to!' he protested.

'That was before Ben was killed. Now all I can think of is getting Manning.'

'You stretched out for Manning.'

'Only because Ben asked me to.' Her eyes glittered as she stared into his rugged face.

'Well Ben didn't ask for you to stretch out for me. You figured to have a little fun on the side with me when Ben wasn't around. He ain't around now, and I ain't gonna do a blame thing until we've been together again.'

'I got news for you, Trig. What we did together was with Ben's blessing. He wanted to keep you sweet so you didn't go off like you sometimes do and spoil a good set-up. You're a little crazy, you know, and Ben was the only one could handle you. He told me to lay for you and that's the only reason I did it. But Ben ain't giving the orders no more, unless they got gangs where he's gone, and you ain't getting near me, Trig. That's a promise. If you figure that's too much for you to bear then go

27

ahead and pull out. Me and Trimble can get along just great. We don't really need you to help us.'

She glanced down the slope to where Trimble was dismounting about two hundred yards away, crouching in the shade of a rock to smoke a cigarette. She moved her horse back from the crest a few feet, returning her gaze to Forbes's harsh features. She could see indecision in his eyes and knew that she could make him obey her, although he was powerful enough to pick her up and almost snap her in two with his massive, cruel hands.

'Better make up your mind to it,' she snapped. 'Time's awasting. You've got a lot of riding to do. I can see that you ain't happy with my refusal, so I'll make a deal with you. The day you hand Chet Manning to me, hogtied and ready for me to do what I want to him, I'll do what you want. That's a promise, and I'll keep it.'

'Now you're just talking to get me to do like you want.' He glanced down at his big hands, flexing the fingers convulsively. 'You know, there's nothing to stop me plugging Trimble where he's sitting right now. That would make you all alone in the world. Then you'd have to do what I said.'

'Go ahead and shoot him if you think it's right. But it'll be too late afterwards to find out that I'm as tough inside as you are. I reckon you know I mean what I say, Trig. We know each other pretty well.'

He looked into her eyes for a long moment, and the silence between them seemed to thicken, to catch at her throat like one of his powerful hands. There was a red glint in his eyes and she knew he was near to madness. At times he ran amok like a loco steer, and she was afraid that her refusal to satisfy him might just tip the balance of his sanity. If he did lose control then he would probably kill her. But she felt that she was on safe ground.

'There's too much at stake right now,' she prompted softly. 'You've got a lot of riding to do, Trig. Make a start now and see what you can turn up. If you do prove to me that you're man enough to step into Ben's boots then I'll think again. That is a fair offer, and it's the best you'll get from me right now. I don't like a man who is all mouth and no action. Prove yourself to me and I'll change my attitude.'

'Hell, if you ain't got a good mind of your own,' he said grudgingly, still clenching and unclenching his big hands. 'But

28

don't take me for a fool, Glory. There are some folks as do, and I've seen the end of them in my time. I'll go along with you just this once, but if you don't come across with your promise the day I give you Chet Manning then you'll be sorry. I'll ride out now. I'll see you back at the hideout in about a week, and don't take any chances riding around this country. Stay low in case there is a posse out. When I get back we'll be in business against Manning. That'll suit you fine, huh?'

He waited but she did not reply, and he shrugged his powerful shoulders and swung into his saddle. He rode away without looking back, and already his mind was fixed upon what he had to do. He was going to take over where Ben Yaro had finished, and planned to do a better job. But only time could tell if he would be able to prove himself without Yaro's guidance.

Chapter Three

Manning spent his first night back in Buffalo Junction in the Blaine house, occupying the room that had belonged to Asa's son Willard. During that evening he sat in the parlour, getting up to date with local news with the family, with Rosa Mozee in their midst, and he began to feel a strong attraction towards the girl. He sensed that Netta did not like having Rosa in the house and eyed Asa's niece critically, recalling the only time he had made love to her. He wanted her again, but there was no love in his mind. Women, to him, were merely sex objects, to be enjoyed whenever possible, and he noted that since his return Netta had been distinctly possessive towards him. That was a woman's way, he knew, and wondered how he could cool her ardour while remaining on the best possible terms with her.

'I figure to go out to end of track tomorrow on the work train, Asa,' he said. 'I want to see Ike again and have a look at the progress that's been made during my absence. Then I'll get down to that other business we discussed.'

Asa nodded, stifling a yawn. He arose, making his apologies. 'I have to be up early in the morning,' he remarked, 'It's time I hit the hay. You're looking tired, Chet, so I suggest you do the same.'

'Yeah, I'm looking forward to my sack.' Manning arose and kissed Aunt Polly's cheek. 'Goodnight, Aunt Polly. Sleep well.'

He caught Netta's eye as he left the room and the girl did not break off her conversation with Rosa, but there was a message in her eyes which Manning could read, and he felt his pulses race as he went up to bed. When he had undressed he sank wearily into the bed and blew out the lamp, his gunbelt and sixgun close to hand on the bed post. He lay in the dark for a long time, thinking about the immediate future, his ears keened for noises within the house. He heard Aunt Polly's voice outside, bidding

Rosa goodnight as she showed the girl into a guest room, and Manning firmed his lips as he considered getting into Rosa's company. But anticipation sent pangs through his chest and stomach and he lay motionless, resting, waiting for Netta, who would surely come to visit him.

The house was silent, the night dark, and he had almost fallen asleep when a furtive sound aroused him and he raised himself on one elbow, peering towards the door. He could see it opening slowly and caught his breath, for if Asa discovered what was going on there would be trouble. The next instant a pale figure came slowly towards the bed.

'Chet, are you still awake?' It was Netta, and her voice was pitched little above a whisper.

'Been waiting for you,' he replied. 'Take off that nightdress and come in here.' He opened the bed, his eyes narrowed as he saw her strip off. The next instant she was with him under the single cover and their naked bodies pressed together. He gathered her gently into his embrace, stroking her face, smoothing the hair from her temples while she pushed herself against his big, powerful frame. He drew his fingers along the side of her face and across her neck, touching her shoulders lightly before permitting his gentle fingers to caress her breasts. She shivered involuntarily as he slipped one hand beneath her shoulders and enveloped her in his embrace. He kissed her gently, trying to contain his passion, but already he was throbbing with powerful male desire, and the soft warmth of her flesh further inflamed him.

The next instant he had let go of his control and dropped upon her receptive flesh. He was heavy and she could scarcely breathe, but he supported himself upon his elbows, easing between her thighs. Her body was flushed with longing. She reached out eager hands for him, and a kind of desperation seized her. But he was kissing her, his mouth moving from one part of her body to another, and she began to tremble with desire, wanting to cry out to him to go on and complete the act. He seemed to be teasing her, tantalising with his movements, but she realised that he needed this contact and forced herself to be patient.

His hands were stroking her back and pressing her thighs, and she could sense his mounting urgency. He was trying to give her the utmost pleasure, yet his own demands could not be denied, and finally he slammed against her, hard and sharp, and she fought down a cry as he penetrated her. Her flesh was willing and ready, giving way to his almost brutal dominance, and she opened her legs wide and twisted convulsively as he went to work upon her, resolutely and with controlled passion. They were like animals, she thought, and yet she loved him madly and was jealous of Rosa, who seemed to be taken up with him, although his manner had betrayed no reciprocal interest to her critical eyes.

Then her mind closed against all thought as pure physical sensation claimed her, and she set her teeth into his shoulder and clawed at his back as she encompassed him and drew the very heart from him with her body. She was afraid that the noise of their love-making would be overheard. Uncle Asa was a light sleeper and Chet's breathing was heavy and laboured, for he was not yet fully fit after his wound. But he evoked powerful responses from her. She quivered, working in time with his own feverish movements. She seemed to be climbing the side of a mountain until she reached the very top, where she clung precariously with eager fingertips, until repletion struck and she seemed to be falling down and down into a black abyss which swallowed her completely. Her teeth met his flesh and she bit hard to prevent an outcry. But he was working powerfully, unsatiated, and she set herself to accommodate him until he was rigid against her for long moments before slumping exhausted upon her damp body.

She held him tightly while he slept, and felt the steady rise and fall of his powerful chest. He was her man and she would never let him go. But they would have to be careful. Uncle Asa had warned her to stay away from Chet. She firmed her lips as she peered into the darkness, and Manning groaned a little, as if reliving a nightmare. But he was sound asleep and she finally eased sideways and left his bed, pulling on her nightdress before moving silently to the door. She could scarcely breathe for fear of getting caught, but reached her room thankfully as the greyness of dawn was peeping into the sky. Then she went to bed and fell asleep instantly, exhausted and happy.

Manning awoke with a start and looked around quickly, afraid that he and Netta had overslept. But the girl was gone and he lay back with a sigh, looking at the first rays of sunlight peering in at the window. He was tired but satisfied, and sat up,

32

looking at the red scar of his most recent bullet wound. It was like a red sore, depressed, ragged around the edges, and situated just below his left collar bone. It hurt him occasionally, but had healed, and he knew that severed nerve ends caused what pain he felt. He thought of what might lay ahead and discovered that there was a cold sensation in the pit of his stomach. He arose hurriedly and dressed, pausing as he buckled his six-gun into place on his right hip. Drawing the weapon, he stared at it as if he had never seen a gun before, and wondered again if his nerve was failing him. He shook his head and left the room, going down the stairs to find Aunt Polly already in the kitchen and preparing breakfast.

He washed out back and then sat at the big wooden table, his mind wandering over the recent past and the near future. When Aunt Polly set his breakfast before him she looked shrewdly at him with experienced brown eyes.

'You're looking far from ready for duty, Chet,' she observed. 'Do you sleep well at nights now or does that last gunfight bother you?'

'I'm all right, Aunt Polly,' he responded, aware that he could not tell her what was sapping his strength. 'How are you making out? Have you got over the shock of losing Willard?'

'I think I always sensed that something would happen to him,' she replied, moving towards the door. 'I'd better make sure Asa is awake, and Rosa will have to be getting up if she's going to make the work-train to end of track.'

'I'm going out there myself this morning,' he responded. 'I can't wait to get back to work.'

Netta came down the stairs while Aunt Polly was absent, and ran across the kitchen to kiss him fervently on the mouth. He looked towards the door, aware that if Asa caught them he could be out of a job and ruin some long-standing friendships. But Netta was here for the taking and he had to have her.

'Be careful,' he said. 'We've had enough trouble without starting some more.'

'Are you going on duty this morning?' she countered.

'I've got to get back into harness.' He nodded. 'I'm going out to end of track.'

'Because Rosa is going out there to see her father?'

'Hey, you sound jealous.' He eyed her closely. 'There's no need for that. You know I have to travel around the district,

3   33

and I need to check end of track before doing anything else. That's the most important part of the project right now.'

'Jake Mullin has been doing all right out there while you've been gone.'

'So I heard. But I am the chief troubleshooter and it's my responsibility to see that everything is working smoothly. If you figure it's wrong for me to accompany Rosa then why don't you ask Aunt Polly if you can come along?'

'I think I'll do that.' She nodded and hurried from the room.

Manning sighed, unable to understand womanly guiles. But he knew that when a man began to show interest in any female she immediately began to think in the long term and started to plan for possession and marriage. That was the last thing he wanted. All he needed was a sympathetic woman to whom he could turn whenever he needed her.

Asa and Rosa came down to breakfast, and Manning eyed Rosa keenly without appearing to do so. Her dark eyes were filled with animation, for she was elated at the thought of seeing her father later. But there was something about her which tugged at Manning's mind. He had always fancied Netta, from the very first moment of meeting her, but he had never felt the desire to become emotionally involved with her. Sex with her was all right, but beyond that he drew the line. But he fancied that he could become quite serious about Rosa Mozee.

'So you're going out to end of track,' Asa commented, tucking into his breakfast. He looked up at Manning. 'Don't be gone too long. I want you to handle that other business we talked about. I figure that's very important right now.'

'I've been thinking about it,' Manning replied, 'and I agree with you. It will have to be settled before I can devote my attention to the railroad.'

'I'm glad you see it my way. Perhaps you'll tell Jake Mullin to carry on as he's doing until he hears different from us. Give my regards to Ike when you see him. He's due for the shock of his life when he sets eyes on Rosa.' Asa transferred his attention to the girl. 'I expect you'll stay out at end of track for a few days, if your pa ain't too busy. But you'll always find shelter in this house when you need it.'

'Thank you,' Rosa replied. 'You're all very kind.'

'You ain't figuring on travelling in those lady clothes, are you?' Manning demanded, studying her green hoopskirt.

'Netta, you and Rosa are about the same size. Ain't you got some Levis and a shirt for her? If she's gonna be travelling on the work train then she'll need to be dressed for the part.'

'Surely.' Netta nodded, pushing aside her plate. 'Come up to my room, Rosa, and I'll see what I've got that will fit you.'

The girls left the room and Asa leaned forward towards Manning.

'Take good care of her until she reaches end of track and her pa,' he advised, 'and watch out for trouble. That trio you need might be aware that you're back, and the kind of thing they'd do is aim to get you with a rifle.'

'I'll keep my eyes open,' Manning promised, finishing his coffee. He arose from the table and stretched, then checked his sixgun. 'This is just like old times, huh? I'm glad to get back, Asa.'

'I'm happy to have you, but I don't like the situation as it is, and I won't be happy until you've nailed that saloon gal and those two hardcases.'

'I'll take care of it,' Manning went to the door and peered out at the day. The sky was cloudless, and the heat was already building up. He slitted his eyes and turned when he heard the voices of the two girls, catching his breath when Rosa appeared, looking somewhat self-conscious in tight-fitting Levis and a shirt. Her feet were thrust into calf-high riding boots, and Netta had found her a lady's low-crowned stetson. 'Now you look the part,' he commented. 'If you're ready we'd better get across to the depot. The work train will be pulling out pretty soon.'

'I've packed a picnic basket for you,' Aunt Polly said. 'It's a mighty long way to end of track now. They must have added another forty miles since you went away, Chet.'

'Forty miles, huh? Well that's not top speed track-laying. But a lot of good, experienced men died out there, huh?' His face showed bitterness for a moment, then he picked up his hat. 'Well I'll go take a look at it. Come on, Rosa.' He took the picnic basket from Aunt Polly, grinned at Netta, who was staying behind, and led Rosa out through the front of the house. They crossed the street to the depot, where the work train was almost ready to pull out. There was a crummy at the rear of the flatcars carrying rails and ties, and Manning led the way to it, ushering Rosa inside. There was no conductor and they had the vehicle to themselves.

'Make yourself comfortable,' Manning said. 'I'm just going along to the engine to have a word with the engineer and the fireman. Later perhaps you'd like to have a ride on the footplate. It's a bit dirty, but that don't matter too much seeing the way you're dressed right now.'

She smiled, shaking her head. 'I never thought I'd see the day when I dressed like a real westerner,' she said. 'These clothes seem so colourful.'

'Mebbe, but they're practical, and that's what counts out here.' Manning chuckled and left the crummy, walking forward along the train until he reached the locomotive. One-Eye Ward was the engineer, and he greeted Manning like a long-lost brother.

'It's great to see you back alive and kicking, Chet,' the engineer said. 'Who's the boy you put into the crummy? Is he gonna work at end of track?'

'That ain't no boy. It's Ike Mozee's daughter, and he doesn't know about her. Has he got a surprise coming to him!'

'Didn't know he had a daughter,' One-Eye retorted. 'Say, you ain't using that as an excuse to trundle along one of them gals you're allus playing around with, are you?'

'One-Eye!' Manning said reproachfully. 'I thought you knew me better than that. But let's get down to business. There's been no trouble around here since we wiped out Yaro, has there?'

'Nothing happened that I know about, although we're allus ready for anything,' came the quick reply.

'Perhaps you'll stop at the site where the big raid took place when we reach it,' Manning continued. 'I'd like to have a look at it.'

'It looks a mess,' the engineer reported. 'Now if you get back in the crummy I'll set this train arolling. If I'm late at end of track Ike will have my other eye.'

Manning nodded and returned to the caboose and, when the train pulled out, he and Rosa stood on the platform at the rear and gazed out across the hot plain. Manning leaned against the rail and watched Buffalo Junction fading into the background before eventually dropping out of sight beyond the horizon, and the gentle motion of the train made him feel sleepy. But Rosa wanted to talk and they sat in the crummy with the doors open to induce a cooling draught and chatted.

Manning confirmed what he suspected as the train travelled

south-west along the new track. He was attracted to this girl as he had not been attracted to any other, including Netta. He found that he could not take his gaze from her features, and the sound of her voice sent a thrill through him. Time passed so quickly that he was surprised when the whistle of the engine attracted his attention, and he went out to the platform to see that they had reached the site of the camp where the big raid had taken place.

They were stopping in a low valley, and on either side of the track lay the wreck of the camp that had been blasted by Yaro's hardcases. An engine lay on its side, devastated by dynamite, and there were bent and twisted rails and blackened piles of ties that had been fired. In the background was a small forest of wooden crosses where the dead had been buried, and Manning jumped to the ground when the train finally stopped.

'You'd better stay where you are,' he said to Rosa as she started to descend. 'We won't be stopping. This is where your pa was shot, and you can see just how many men lost their lives in the big raid. I want to go and pay my respects to them.'

He set off alone for the small graveyard of five rows each containing ten crosses. He walked along them, reading the names and putting faces to them, and blamed himself for this tragedy. He had been so certain that Ben Yaro would not strike at the construction camp, but a herd of stampeding cattle had changed everything. A shuddering sigh escaped him and he walked back to the train, his eyes bright and his teeth clenched. One-Eye Ward tooted on the whistle as he swung aboard the caboose, and they jolted forward once more.

Manning was silent after that, standing on the platform and gazing at the wreckage until it dropped from sight. They passed several other small areas of wreckage, where the outlaws had struck at the graders out in front of the main construction camp, and he kept sighing as he recalled all the brave men who had given their blood along with their sweat so that the railroad could be completed.

The whistle sounded about an hour later, and Manning leaned out from the side of the crummy to see that they were approaching end of track. S & W had really pulled itself up by its bootstraps, he thought, judging by the track that had been laid since the disaster. But railroaders were tough men and there was not much that could halt them for long.

'You'd better let me have a few words with your pa before you jump out at him,' he said to Rosa, and she smiled, although she seemed nervous.

'I hope he'll be pleased to see me,' she countered. 'I don't think I'll even know what he looks like, it's been so long.'

'Well it's a fact that he won't know you,' Manning retorted, and swung to the ground as the train came to a halt.

He looked around, pleased to see such a buzz of industry, and there was Ike Mozee's coach standing on the small loop-line. He glanced at Rosa, motioning for her to follow him, and she stayed at his back as he walked towards the coach, where he could see Mozee's trestle table beside the track, the maps and papers upon it weighted down against the hot breeze.

Mozee was standing at the table, accompanied by a couple of his foremen, and they were studying the maps. Mozee was talking forcefully, thumping the table from time to time, and Manning smiled, for this was typical of the construction camp boss. But his gaze was critical as he looked at his friend and he could see that Mozee had lost some weight. The man was a redhead, squat and powerfully built, with massive arms. But it was easy to see that the wound he had received in the camp raid had brought him down low.

He turned and spotted Manning, grinning immediately; he left the two foremen and came forward with outstretched hand.

'Chet, am I glad to see you! How are you, son? I heard tell you was pretty hard hit.'

'That's what they told me about you, Ike.' Manning grasped the big hand and shook it warmly. 'But I figured you'd be okay. The bullet ain't been made yet that could take you out.'

'I could say the same about you.' Mozee smiled. His face was pale beneath its tan and his clothes seemed to hang rather loosely on him.

'You look like you been through the mill though,' Manning said. 'You didn't come back to work too soon, did you, Ike?'

'Of course I did! That's what you're doing, aren't you?' Mozee grinned, but his features sobered when he saw Rosa standing in the background. 'A girl,' he commented. 'You brung her along, Chet? You know the rule about women around the construction camp.'

'Sure I brought her. You didn't want me to leave her behind in Buffalo Junction, did you? I figured she would be safe under my protection until I got her here. Now she is here I'm handing her over to you. Can you put her up in your coach, Ike?'

'Are you crazy?' Mozee demanded. 'I can't have a woman around here.'

'She ain't just any woman,' Manning countered.

'She wouldn't be, knowing you.'

'You could be polite to her. What about a drink? She ought not be out in this heat. Let's go into your coach and we can talk, or, rather, I'll let you take her into your coach and you can talk to her.'

'Please, Chet,' Rosa said, and Manning nodded, his face sobering.

'Sorry, Rosa,' he said, 'but I just couldn't resist having a go at Ike.' He looked Mozee in the eyes. 'You heard me call her Rosa,' he said. 'You ever know anyone by that name?'

Mozee shook his head slowly, his greenish eyes blank. 'It doesn't ring a bell,' he admitted. 'Should I know her?'

'You ought to.' Manning was enjoying himself. 'Her first name is Rosa. Supposing I tell you her second name is Mozee? Does that help at all?'

Mozee's face tightened and he peered intently into Rosa's face. The girl seemed to cringe, but Manning reached out a large hand and placed it upon her shoulder.

'Rosa Mozee!' Ike said cautiously.

'None other!' Manning chuckled. 'She's your daughter, Ike.'

Mozee seemed to turn pale, and he tottered as if his balance had been upset. But his eyes bored into the girl's face and then he nodded slowly.

'I can see your mother in you, Rosa,' he said a little unsteadily. 'Do you recognise me at all?'

'Yes, Father. Mother had a photograph of you. You look a bit older now, but I'd have known you anywhere.'

'Take her into the coach and talk privately,' Manning said. 'I want to have a few words with Jake Mullin. I can see him over there. I'll come back to you presently, Ike.' He smiled at Rosa. 'I told you he wasn't so bad, didn't I?'

She smiled, and Ike reached out and took her elbow. Manning watched them enter the coach, then sighed heavily and turned

39

away. Unaccustomed emotion burned in him for a few moments as he went to talk to his chief assistant. Jake Mullin had spotted him and was coming forward, but Manning kept his mind off railroad matters for a few seconds longer while he thought of Rosa. He knew that when he began to check out the camp he would become embroiled in the situation once more, and it was something he was dreading.

Chapter Four

Trig Forbes pulled his hatbrim lower over his pale eyes and glanced up at the sun as he wiped sweat from his forehead. He had searched for signs of the three hardcases he wished to recruit in the wilderness north of Gadson Flats, checking out some of the hideouts he knew, and although he had found signs of recent habitation in some of them he did not come across the tough trio. There were two more places he intended checking before giving them up as a bad job, but first he needed supplies and water. He knew the country well and figured to drop in on a small horse rancher situated in a valley near by. The place was a regular stop-over for owl-hooters and those who rode the back trails, and he pushed his horse steadily, alert as always, aware that the local law would be on the watch for him. There might even be posses out looking for him.

As he rode he considered the situation, and the more he thought about bossing a big gang the better he liked the idea. He was a massively-built man, strong and stubborn, primitive and passionate, and there was a twist in his mind which had robbed him of all human compunction. He obeyed the simple law of a predatory animal – take what was needed. He needed Glory with a burning ferocity which no amount of thinking or changing the subject could assuage, and the longer he thought about her the more he lusted for her. He pictured her trim figure and grinned, aware that, having tasted the fruits of her body, he could not prevent his hunger from blossoming. His harsh mouth did not relax as he continued, and there was a flame of desire in his narrowed eyes.

Towards nightfall he topped a rise and reined up, peering into the growing shadows and grinning when he saw the stark outlines of ranch buildings clustered together by a creek. The last of the day's sun glinted upon the flat expanse of water and he eased his bulk in the saddle and drew a long breath as he fought the strange restlessness which filled him. It was Glory, he thought angrily. Her tantalising image in his mind was disturbing him, made him all too aware of his powerful body, and his all-consuming appetites could not be held under control. If he'd had the time he would have ridden for Gadson Flats, where he had a Mexican woman waiting for him, but there were more important things to be done and he obeyed his crooked instincts, although frustration simmered in him and made him as dangerous as a barrel of gunpowder in a burning shack.

He approached the ranch cautiously. Slim Turner, the rancher, was sympathetic towards outlaws, partly because it would have been suicide to show hostility and partly because Yaro had paid well for supplies and information, and this dried range could barely support the stock Turner could afford to run.

Forbes approached and dismounted at the back of the house, moving in on foot towards the kitchen window, which showed as a yellow square in the night. He was hungry and thirsty, having used the last of his supplies the day before, and his hunger made him as dangerous as a starving wolf. If the law were here then he would fight in a blind fury.

But the ranch was quiet, although a lantern gleamed in the barn, and Forbes moved in against the rear wall of the building, easing forward to peer through the window. His tongue licked around his dry lips when he saw a woman cooking at the stove. It was Abbie, Turner's wife, a big, strong female in her thirties. She was not pretty. Her way of life had coarsened her considerably, but she was a woman, and Forbes drew a deep breath as passion flickered into life inside him. He watched her with a glitter in his pale eyes, thinking of Glory, then he heard a small sound in the distance and instantly became a calculating animal.

The sound came from the barn, and Forbes moved in that direction, his hands near to the butts of his holstered guns. Slim Turner and his teenage son would be around somewhere. It was almost time for supper. His mouth watered, but now he needed more than supper! He reached the side of the barn and peered through a convenient knothole. Two figures were inside one of the stalls, bending over a sick horse that was covered with a blanket. Forbes grinned tightly, his eyes glint-

42

ing, and there was a curious tremor deep inside him.

Slim Turner straightened from the side of the horse and looked at his son Chad. Turner was forty-five, his son almost twenty, and the youngster's mother had died giving birth to the boy. Abbie had come to the ranch six years earlier as a housekeeper, and Turner eventually married her.

'Son, I reckon you better go saddle up and ride for Doc Hollis. We're gonna lose this mare if we're not careful.'

'Okay, Pa. But it'll be after midnight before I get back.'

'That's okay! Don't kill your own hoss, Chad!'

Forbes eased back and made his way to the corral, and he was crouching in the shadows of the pole fence as Chad Turner appeared. When the youngster paused to slide out the loose poles that covered the entrance to the corral, Forbes straightened and sprang like a mountain lion, his heavy left hand clamping over the youngster's mouth to prevent an outcry, his right hand clutching his long-bladed hunting knife, stabbing swiftly, expertly. Chad Turner died instantly and Forbes crouched over the lifeless boy, wiping the blade of his knife on the youngster's shirt front as he peered around, breathing heavily, filled with the savage glee of an Indian on the warpath.

Moving back to the barn, Forbes entered and approached Slim Turner, who turned as his keen ears caught the sound of boots scraping the hard ground.

'Something wrong, Chad?' he began, then started at sight of Forbes's massive figure. 'Trig Forbes!' he rasped. 'Hell, you gave me a start! Where did you come from? Do you know there's been a posse around here looking for you?'

'I guess there would be, Slim.' Forbes's voice was husky, and tremors of anticipation were darting through him as he thought of the woman in the house. 'I dropped in for food and drink. You seen anything of Hemp Arrel and his two side-kicks? I been looking for several days.'

'Saw them last week. From what I heard, they're planning to quit the country. Now Yaro and the others are gone they reckon the law will be too strong for them around here. Chet Manning is making the railroad too tough a proposition.'

'I got a job for them.' Forbes paused at Turner's side, eyeing the man. Turner felt the intensity of the hard gaze and looked up into Forbes's shadowed face as the bigger man sledged his right fist into the rancher's stomach.

Turner gasped and bent over, and Forbes set his teeth into his bottom lip as a fierce joy flared in his mind. He chopped his left fist against the back of Turner's neck, dropping the man as if he had been poleaxed, then kicked viciously when Turner lay motionless. A growl tore itself loose from Forbes's throat and he bent and seized Turner by the neck as an insane rage flooded him. He dragged the man off the ground and strangled him with powerful hands that squeezed remorselessly. He gripped Turner's neck while sweat ran down his face, and even after he knew Turner was dead he did not relax. He growled like a bear wakened from hibernation and shook the nerveless body.

It was the woman's voice calling out in the darkness that brought him out of the paroxysm that gripped him.

'Come and get it!'

Forbes shivered and relaxed his large hands. Turner's body slid limply to the hard-packed ground. A great sigh tore from Forbes's lips and he got to his feet, flexing his hands as he moved to the door. He peered out across the yard and saw the door of the house closing as the woman went back to her cooking. Moving stealthily, he went around to the back door, peering in again through the window, noting the three places that had been set at the big wooden table. His lips slackened as he stared at the woman, and a throbbing pain hit the pit of his stomach.

Pushing open the door, he entered the kitchen, and Abbie Turner looked up, showing momentary fear as her gaze alighted upon his fearsome figure.

'Trig Forbes! You gave me quite a start. Slim is out in the barn with Chad. I just called them to supper. They're nursing a sick horse.'

'I just seen them! Slim told me to come on in and get some grub. I need a sack of supplies too!'

'Do you want to wash up?' she demanded, and paused as he shook his head. Her keen eyes studied his heavy figure, and she suppressed a pang of fear, a quick shiver of premonition. She had never liked the comings and goings of the outlaws who used the place as a stop-over. But it was none of her business, and they paid well for the service they received. But of all the bad-men who came and went, Trig Forbes was the one who scared her most. Now she studied him, trying to gauge his mood, and

44

saw fresh blood on his shirt front. 'Have you been hurt?' she demanded.

He glanced down at the bloodstain and grinned.

'It ain't mine,' he retorted.

'Well sit down and I'll feed you!' She went to the stove but Forbes shook his head.

'Leave that food. I'll eat Slim's.' He reached out and dragged the big plate across the table, sitting where he could watch her, and saw that she glanced anxiously at the door. He noted her uneasiness and figured to allay her suspicions until after he had eaten. He got to work on the supper, speaking with a full mouth. 'Slim is sending Chad into town for the Doc. That hoss must be something, the way they're fussing over it. They won't be coming in yet!'

She sighed heavily and took up the third plate, putting it into the oven, and Forbes watched her while he shovelled food into his mouth. Gravy dribbled down his chin and soaked into his dusty shirt. When she came to sit opposite he leered at her, and barely overcame the impulse to reach out and grab her. He savoured the sense of anticipation that thrilled through him, working his jaws stolidly as he filled the gnawing emptiness in his belly.

Towards the end of the meal the woman began to grow restive. Twice she looked at Forbes but he pretended not to notice. Then she got to her feet.

'I'd better go out there and tell them to come in for supper,' she remarked. 'It's spoiling.'

'Got any whisky?' he countered, pushing aside his plate. He picked at his teeth with a dirty thumbnail.

She went through to a front room and returned moments later with a bottle and a glass. As she set it down upon the table beside him Forbes reached up and grasped her wrist. She paused and looked into his face, instinctively aware of what was passing through his mind. Her intuition warned that he was more than ordinarily dangerous.

'Let go of me!' she said firmly. 'Slim will gutshoot you if you don't behave.'

'Not Slim!' He snickered harshly. 'I figure he must be stiff as a board now!'

She stared into his eyes, noting the blaze in their pale depths, and fear crept into her mind.

45

'What have you done?' she demanded, her tone growing shrill. 'Where's Slim?'

'In hell now, I reckon, knowing Slim.' Forbes got to his feet, towering over her, taking her by the shoulders.

Still she could not, or would not, grasp his meaning, and shook her head worriedly.

'You haven't hurt him, have you?' she asked fearfully.

'I killed him! Strangled the life out of him.'

She cried out incoherently, her face blanching with shock. Then she twisted in his grasp and snatched up a knife from the table. Forbes laughed and dashed it from her hand, sending it tinkling halfway across the kitchen. She cringed from him, sensing his intentions. His eyes seemed to have a red glint in their depths as the lamplight filled them.

'Chad?' she whispered.

'His blood on my shirt! He never knew what hit him.'

'Why? We've always been friendly towards you.'

'You!' he rasped. 'I want you.'

She began to struggle but he swept her off her feet, tucking her under his left arm, ignoring her ineffectual struggles. He thrust a lamp into her hand, then snatched up the bottle of whisky, and eased through the door to mount the stairs to Turner's bedroom. When they entered the room he set down the bottle, took the lamp from her, then threw her upon the bed.

'You and me have got a right busy night ahead of us,' he said. 'Don't give me no trouble because I ain't in the mood. Just do like I say and you might live to see the sun come up tomorrow.'

She lay still on the bed, her face set in a mask of shock, but when he moved threateningly towards her she sprang off the bed and darted towards the door, trying to elude his outstretched hand. Forbes chuckled and grabbed a handful of her hair, pulling her to the floor, and although she struggled with all the strength of her powerful body she was helpless in his massive hands. He seized her dress by the collar and ripped it away from her body, revealing full breasts and fleshy hips.

He threw her across the bed, his powerful, hairy arms holding her, and the feel of her flesh brought him to lustful readiness. He backed off, stripping off his own clothes, keeping an eye on her in case she tried to get away. He placed his gunbelts where he could reach them quickly but she could not, and when he was naked he hurled himself upon her, his fingers digging cruelly into her flesh. She tried to claw his face and he slapped her hard with the back of his left hand, then he thrust her hands above her head, forcing a knee between her legs and kneeling over her.

'Now you just quieten down or you're gonna get hurt,' he warned, his voice husky with lust. 'I need to be pleasured, and I ain't gonna let you spoil things for me. You'll do whatever I want or suffer for not doing it.'

He forced her feet around his waist and slid his left hand under her buttocks, raising her body easily from the bed, sliding his hand into position in order to guide her pelvis towards his erect member. He did not move but dragged her towards him, then thrust with his hips to penetrate her. She cried out and he chuckled evilly, his eyes glittering. When he was inside he bent over her, flattening his massive body over hers, pinning her down with his weight. She bit him, tried to claw him, and he chuckled happily.

'Go to it,' he cursed. 'I like a woman who'll fight. Get away from me if you can. But whatever you do, you're gonna know you've had a man by the time I get done with you.'

The woman was powerless in his hands and he thrust violently at her, lust shining in his eyes, a merciless grin upon his stubbled face. He began to hammer relentlessly, caught up by his own consuming passions. He reached a climax and shuddered against her, then lay replete for long minutes, reaching out for the whisky bottle without leaving her. When she thought he was about to fall asleep he roused up and started over again, working like a stockyard bull, and so it went on through the night. He dozed little but often, until dawn finally came, but he needed to perform the act yet again before he was satisfied that he could get through the next week without another woman.

As the sun came up he kicked her out of the bed and ordered her to get breakfast. He dressed as she dressed, and they went down to the kitchen together. She prepared food under his watchful gaze, and when he had eaten his fill he made her sack up some provisions and fill a canteen. Then came the moment of departure.

She stood before him, frozen in shock, grey-faced and incoherent, and Forbes sneered as he gazed at her. He drew his sixgun and thumbed a shot at her, catching her in the breast, and as she slumped to the floor he turned on his heel and strode

47

out. He left his horse in the corral and took a fresh animal, mounting up to ride for the mountains without looking back. The little ranch lay brooding in the sunlight of the new day, silent and still, filled with the atmosphere of death.

Forbes was tired as he rode, but the aching frustration in his mind was gone and he could think of Glory without the terrible squeezing sensation that usually gripped him. He narrowed his eyes as he thought of the previous night. His breathing quickened and he clenched his hands. He had to make a good haul so he could leave the area and set himself up in a fine hideout with plenty of liquor and several women. His eyes glittered as he made plans. But he needed help. He could not handle it alone.

Two days later he rode into one of Delmont's old hideouts and saw three horses in a pole corral. A low whistle sounded as he appeared, and he saw a rifle barrel poke out of the window of the ramshackle cabin standing drunkenly under a rock overhang. He grinned, recognising the horses. He had found Hemp Arrel and his two sidekicks.

A man appeared in the doorway of the shack and another showed himself from the front left corner, both holding rifles, while the long gun covering Forbes from the window was still apparent.

'Howdy, Hemp!' Forbes called. 'You sure hid yourself out! I been looking several days for signs of you.' He rode right up to the cabin and dismounted, slapping dust from his shirt and pants before adjusting the heavy cartridge belts buckled around his thick waist.

'Trig Forbes!' Arrel grinned tightly, his expression relaxing although his grey eyes did not lose their wariness. He was around forty, but looked a lot younger, and his tall, heavymuscled body was in good physical shape. His face was dark, weathered by an outdoor life, his mouth tight and mirthlessly smiling. But inside he was hard and cold. He never liked or trusted Forbes. They had ridden together years before on the Texas border and, tough as he was, Hemp Arrel had drawn the lines at some of the deeds Trig Forbes committed. But there was nothing in his manner to make this attitude apparent, and he was careful not to show any emotion as he studied the massive figure now standing before him.

'Glad I caught up with you, Hemp!' Forbes glanced at the

stocky, dark-faced man standing by the front corner of the cabin. 'Hi, Ben! Glad to see you around!'

Ben Santor lowered his rifle and came forward, a grin on his greasy face. He was bowlegged, dressed in dirty, ragged range clothes, and his fleshy face was covered with black stubble.

'How'd you get out of jail, Trig?' Santor demanded. He stood his rifle against the front wall of the cabin and moved away from it, but his right hand did not stray far from the butt of his holstered sixgun, and there were eight notches on its butt-plates to testify to his prowess.

'Friends of mine busted me out!' Forbes glanced towards the window, where the rifle still covered him. 'Come on out of there, Snap. I got a deal to put to you boys. Now Yaro is gone I need some men around me to help take over this area. Come out and listen to what I have to say.'

Snap Dillon emerged from the cabin, a tall, thin, sharp-tempered man in his middle-thirties. His long face had high, protruding cheekbones. His expression was sour. His blue eyes held a cynical glitter as they regarded Forbes's big figure. He leaned a thin shoulder against a doorpost and remained silent.

'Tough luck on you, Trig, the way Yaro and the others got it,' Arrel remarked, hitching up his gunbelt. 'But we warned you that Chet Manning was hell on wheels. He chewed up our bunch plenty good in Mexico and took back the dough we stole from the railroad.'

Drawing a heavy breath, Forbes held it for a moment, then exhaled sharply. 'That's all history now, and you boys don't have to quit the country. You'd like to get back at Manning, wouldn't you?'

'Let's go in out of the sun,' Arrel said patiently. 'We'll hear your deal, Trig. It was Yaro who figured there wasn't enough pickings around here for all of us, but as I remember it, you tried to get us into the gang.' He grinned harshly. 'As it turned out, we're lucky Yaro was against us, but I reckon I owe you a favour, Trig, and if you're alone now then we might be able to work something out.'

'I ain't alone,' Forbes announced as they entered the cabin, and Arrel produced a bottle of whisky. They sat down and Ben Santor picked up a pack of cards.

'We don't have a lot of time, Hemp,' Snap Dillon cut in. 'We got to be riding if we're gonna get that job done.'

4

'You boys got something on?' Forbes asked eagerly.

'The bank in Gadson Flats!' Arrel remarked. 'You want to cut yourself a piece of that cake, Trig? It's safer than hitting the railroad.'

'I need some dough, and quick,' Forbes retorted. He nodded. 'Yeah! Count me in.'

'A quarter share!' Arrel spoke without hesitation. 'You figuring us four could work together around here now Yaro is gone? Is that what's on your mind?'

'That's it! I reckon we could clean up. Yaro made some mistakes towards the end. He was always filled with liquor and couldn't see straight more than half the time. It had to come, the way he went down, and he was a fool for taking some good men with him.'

'He was mostly successful!' Arrel commented. 'He always managed to hit paydirt when he went for a train.'

'Inside information,' Forbes said.

'Can you still get the same kind of information?' Arrel's eyes glinted until Forbes shook his head.

'The whole set-up got busted when Manning cleaned up. We got to start from scratch.'

'What about Chet Manning?' Ben Santor demanded in a gruff tone. 'He's hell on wheels with a gun and got the Devil's own luck. That's a combination hard to beat. There ain't anyone can take him and get away with it.'

'You don't have to worry about Manning!' Forbes chuckled harshly. 'The friend who busted me and Trimble out of the Buffalo Junction jail is burning to kill Manning, and she'll do it, too.'

'Who's that?' Arrel asked.

'Glory Harpe.' Forbes's eyes glittered.

'Ben Yaro's widow!' Arrel shook his head slowly. 'You expect a woman to take care of Chet Manning? Hell, she set him up for Creed and Penner, and they both cashed their chips!'

'With Trimble's help she'll do it,' Forbes insisted. 'She's cut up about Yaro getting it, and when you see her you'll agree that she means business. I figure with her and Trimble on Manning's trail we can do as we damn well please around the railroad.'

50

'Let's see how our job in Gadson Flats pans out,' Arrel suggested. 'We're riding now, Trig. Come along and pick up a share, and afterwards we'll go into this. If Chet Manning is wiped out then we could really clean up before they get a new chief troubleshooter. I'm interested, Trig! Yaro was no fool most of the time and he hit this area for good reasons. Western Pacific were paying him so I heard. Now if we could take over that contract it would be something. We were gonna pull this one bank job then quit, but, as you say, now Yaro is gone there's room for us.'

Forbes nodded and they prepared to ride out towards Gadson Flats, reaching the outskirts of the town after noon, and while they waited out the last minutes of the time Arrel had planned, they talked. Forbes watched the main street, grinning to himself when he remembered the way he had been busted out of jail back in Buffalo Junction. Then it was time to go and they rode in separately, Forbes taking the back lots and leaving his horse in the alley beside the bank. His face was too well known for him to risk using the street. He went on foot to the front end of the alley and joined Arrel as the outlaw started across the sidewalk to the bank. Ben Santor joined them and they went inside.

There were no customers in the bank at that hour, and the teller was almost dozing in his cage. He woke up abruptly when Forbes stuck a gun under his nose, and the robbery went off without a hitch. Snap Dillon was outside on the sidewalk to cover their escape, and there was a heavy silence hanging over the town.

It was when they were leaving that trouble started. Forbes departed first, carrying a bulging gunny sack and, as he passed the waiting Dillon, he glanced around the deserted street and caught a glimpse of the town marshal hurrying towards the bank. There was a gun in Hart Loman's hand, and Forbes cursed, thumbing off a shot at the marshal. He started running for the alley, and boots pounding the boardwalk told him that the others were also making for their horses.

As he turned into the alley, Forbes glanced over his shoulder, grinning when he saw that Loman was down. But there was a tall figure farther back, running forward with a gun in his hand, and blue smoke eddied as shooting continued. Forbes cursed and ran harder. It was Chet Manning, and Forbes suddenly realised that Manning bothered him more than he cared to admit.

He knew a spasm of real fear as he ran to his horse, mounted, then split the breeze across the back lots.

When he was in the clear he reined up to check, and saw three riders making it away in another direction. He grinned then. It looked as if they had got away! But there would be a pursuit and he rode on, returning to the hideout where he had found Arrel and the others. He felt a sense of relief. The bank raid had been successful and that augured well for the future. All he had to do was get Trimble and Glory worked up so they would ride out to ambush Manning. Then there would be no holding this new gang. If anyone in the area figured Yaro's gang had been tough then they hadn't seen anything yet!

Chapter Five

Manning had a long chat with Jake Mullin, his chief assistant, and learned that all was well. There had been no major incidents since Yaro's gang was wiped out. Mullin, medium-sized, stocky, solidly built, with clear blue eyes and an open face, was happy to see Manning looking so well. But Manning brushed aside all talk of his health.

'Jake, what can you tell me about Glory Harpe and the two outlaws she busted out of jail?' he demanded. 'You know I can't let them go running around loose. They've got to be picked up.'

'Yeah, I know. But while I've devoted all my time to end of track and the way south-west, I've had men out looking for that trio. I know they spell bad trouble, and we've got to get them. But I got something else on my mind, Chet, that you better hear about. Asa took on three new troubleshooters to bring us up to strength. One of them you know very well – Joe Carver. He's over to Hobbsburg right now, and doing well. He and the other two are due back at Buffalo Junction any day. One of the other two is a man named Bolden, Hank Bolden, and I don't like him. It's nothing I can put my finger on; you know that feeling. It's a hunch. I reckon you'd better check him out good, Chet.'

'Okay. I'll look into it when I get back to town. But what about Western Pacific? Are they gonna let us get to Apache Pass first?'

'Are you kidding?' Mullen shook his head slowly, his eyes hooded, filled with worry. 'We've got another month of laying track before we'll be within striking distance of the Pass, and if Western Pacific let us get that far without more trouble then I'll eat my hat. They've done everything in the book so far to stop us, and I can't see them pulling out now.'

'That's what I figure. Mebbe Glory and these other two are gonna get a new gang around them and continue where Yaro left off, huh? What do you think about that?'

'Yaro was the best.' Mullin shook his head. 'I don't think anyone else can handle the deal as well as he did.'

'And look where he is now!' Manning smiled tightly. 'That doesn't say much for the chances of Western Pacific. But I agree with you, Jake. There's nothing I can tell you except be on your guard. I want to get out of here myself and be right on the spot for the last run to the Pass itself, but I got the feeling that Glory Harpe and Trig Forbes might start something that could snowball into bad trouble. I'll have to go out after them. There's no other way. I don't want to, but I got to.'

'I agree with you, and from what I've heard, Asa is of the same mind, ain't he?'

'Yeah. He told me that you're to carry on as you are doing and I've got to get Glory Harpe out of my hair.'

'Rather you than me.' Mullin grinned. 'Are you going back to Buffalo Junction on the work train?'

'Yeah. I guess I'd better see what Ike's gonna do about his daughter. That work train will be ready to roll again in about an hour. Are there any shortages you're worried about, Jake? Anything I can look into before I go?'

'Nope. Asa is taking care of us real well now.' Mullin grinned. 'That raid on the old camp sure woke up a lot of people to the fact that we're really up against it out here. You take care of yourself, Chet, okay?'

'Sure thing.' Manning nodded. 'If you get any sniff of trouble then send a wire right away. Don't take any chances, Jake.'

'You betcha!' Mullin nodded. 'Now I'll have to be going, Chet. I'm riding on ahead to scout out the lie of the land. With that trio on the loose there's no telling what they might try to get up to.'

'I'll get them.' Manning spoke through clenched teeth. 'We'll get rid of them like we get shot of everyone who tries to take us.'

'Be seeing you then. Keep your hand close to your gun.'

Manning nodded, watching his assistant depart. Then he turned and went to Mozee's coach, mounting the steps and tapping at the door. Mozee called out an invitation to enter

54

and Manning did so, to find father and daughter seated in Mozee's office.

'What do you think of my daughter, Chet?' Mozee demanded, smiling cheerfully. His eyes were filled with warmth and a sigh gusted from him.

'She's a credit to you, but I figure you should have made contact with her before.' Manning lounged on a corner of the desk. 'What are your plans for the next few days, Rosa?'

'I don't know.' The girl looked at her father. 'I'd like to stay just to look around and see what life is like out here.'

'No.' Ike shook his head. 'This ain't a fit place for a gal like you, Rosa. And I'm working a full day now so I won't be able to spare any time for you. The best thing you can do is go back to town when Chet does and stay at the Blaine house. Aunt Polly will keep an eye on you, and I'll come into town whenever I can to see you.'

'That sounds sensible to me,' Manning agreed.

'All right.' Rosa sounded unconvinced, but there was a brightness in her eyes as she looked into Manning's face, and he felt a pang cut through him as he gazed into her attractive features. He felt Ike's gaze upon him and met the man's keen eyes.

'I've warned Rosa about you, Chet,' Ike said, a half-grin on his lips. 'She knows you're hell on women, so I want to tell you to walk softly around her, okay?'

Manning held up his hands in mock despair. 'That ain't fair, Ike, and you know it. I'm always a perfect gentleman around any girl.'

'Sure.' Ike nodded. 'But remember that I know you, huh?'

'I reckon it's time to get back to the train.' Manning stood up, dropping a hand to his holstered gun to check it. 'I'm gonna take a ride around the entire area to look out for that trio who are supposed to be looking for me,' he said. 'I'll see Rosa safely back to Buffalo Junction.'

'I'll be coming into town at the end of the week,' Ike said. 'I'll see you then, Rosa.'

The girl nodded, and kissed her father's cheek. They left the coach and walked to the work train, which was being unloaded by a gang of men who swarmed over it like ants, removing the supplies, which were being checked by the foreman. They waited until the train was ready, then boarded it, and Rosa waved goodbye to her father as they pulled out on the return journey.

When they were out of sight of the camp, Manning led Rosa into the crummy and they sat down. He eyed her steadily and she met his gaze.

'I wouldn't pay too much attention to what your father tells you about me,' he said with a careless smile.

'But I have my reputation to consider,' she countered, and there was a gleam in her eyes which made him aware that she was light-hearted.

'I wouldn't try anything on with you. You're the daughter of a good friend of mine.'

'So I'm to miss out on some pleasure just because you know my father!'

'I don't know how to take that remark.'

'You're a very handsome man, Chet.' She smiled, but there was a gleam in her eyes. Then she sobered. 'But what about Netta?'

'Netta?' He frowned. 'What about her?'

'You know that she is in love with you?'

'Netta?' he repeated, frowning more deeply. 'I think she hero-worships me a bit.'

'That's putting it mildly. She's head over heels in love with you.'

'But I have this reputation, for some reason or other, and Uncle Asa has warned me against having anything to do with her.'

'As my father warned me.' Rosa smiled. 'There must be something very potent about you if so many men are concerned about their womenfolk when you're around.'

'You know what reputations are.' He smiled. 'I only wish I was half the man most stories make me out to be.'

'I'm sure there's a lot in your reputation which is true,' she accused. 'But I'm talking about your exploits.'

'I think it's about time to change the subject,' he said, grinning. 'Anyway, you're safe with me around. I've proved that, haven't I?'

'I don't know how to answer that,' she replied.

He was thoughtful during the rest of the trip back to town, and when they alighted in Buffalo Junction he knew that his feelings towards her were settling firmly in a groove. He was attracted to her because she was a pretty girl, but it seemed to go much deeper than that, and when he left her at the depot to make her own way to the Blaine house while he went to Asa's office, his thoughts went with her.

He was hard put to answer Asa's questions on what he thought about the situation at the end of track, and Asa studied him intently, wondering about the indecision showing in his eyes. He wisely refrained from broaching the subject which automatically came to mind for he could remember his own early days when he had acted as a troubleshooter. He had suffered the same doubt and self-searching which was obviously taking place in Manning's mind. But he also knew that the very next time Manning pulled a gun in defence of his life or railroad property the doubts would vanish – unless Manning had lost his nerve completely. That was a possibility which could not be discounted, and he knew a momentary pang as he considered the fact. There would be no way of finding out until that moment of truth came, and then it would be too late. Chet Manning might die in a shoot-out or ambush instead of reacting as he had done in the past.

'I want you to stick around town for a couple of days until I get news in from all over the area,' Asa said. 'And the three new troubleshooters I took on in your absence will be coming into town to report. I want you to get to know them, and let me know what you think of them. One of them you do know well – Joe Carver.'

'Yeah, Jake told me about Joe. It'll be fine working with him again.'

'So stick close to town until I've got situation reports from all over. If we can find out where Glory Harpe and the two hardcases were last seen then you'll know where to begin your job.'

'Okay, if that's the way you want it. I reckon Jake has everything under control out at end of track, so I won't be missed for a couple of weeks. But I need to get out there soon as I can because in the next month we're gonna be within striking distance of Apache Pass, and I don't trust Western Pacific.'

'It'll work out.' Asa got to his feet. 'Come on, let's get over to the house. I can tell by my stomach that it's almost time to eat.'

Manning nodded. He had spent a pleasant day in Rosa's company, but he knew he had to be careful where she was concerned, and he could not afford to give Netta cause for jealousy. If Netta was really in love with him then he would have to watch his step. He could not afford entanglements or complications, and he didn't want to cause any hurt to either girl.

Joe Carver rode into Buffalo Junction the next day, a tall, thin, fair-haired man of twenty-eight who had transferred from a northern area of the railroad. Manning had worked with him on several occasions, finding him dependable and unruffled in any tight situation. He entered Asa's office, covered in dust, gaunt and tight-lipped. Manning was there alone, day-dreaming a little in the heat, trying to forget the past and fighting against the inclination to go and see Rosa at the house. He looked up swiftly as Carver's tall figure darkened the office and got to his feet quickly, advancing with outstretched hand.

'Joe!' he exclaimed. 'I'm real glad to see you! How'd you make out at Hobbsburg?'

'Howdy, Chet,' Carver responded. 'I got my man. He's in jail now, and I recovered the freight that was stolen. I'm sure glad you're back. I've been looking forward to working with you ever since I got into the area. Pity you finished off Ben Yaro before I arrived.'

Manning smiled, motioning Carver to a seat. The tall man sat down, removing his hat, rasping the fingers of his left hand through the stubble on his gaunt face. His smile lingered and there was a bright light in his blue eyes.

'I'm glad Yaro is finished,' Manning retorted. 'He ran us ragged for a while. But we're fairly quiet now and I hope it will stay like that for a spell. I've been waiting for you or one of the others to show up, Joe. I want to make a trip around the area, but I wouldn't leave until at least one of you showed. Do you know either of the other two men Asa engaged?'

'Only their names.' Carver produced a long thin cigar and lit it. He puffed contentedly for a moment, his pale eyes regarding Manning, taking in the store suit, white shirt and neatly-fastened tie. 'Hank Bolden has a bit of a rep, though. He's a tough man who believes in bringing them in dead rather than alive.'

'You've got to be tough to handle this job.' Manning's lips pinched together.

'Yeah, but you don't kill a man who's lifted mebbe a crate of supplies from a boxcar, do you?'

'You don't like Bolden, Joe!' There was a soft note in Manning's voice. 'Why not? What do you know about him?'

'It ain't for me to say.' Carver's slender shoulders lifted then sagged. He smiled sardonically. 'It takes all kinds to run a railroad and keep it free of trouble. But I know you well and I figure you better have advanced warning. Watch out for Bolden!'

'Thanks, Joe. Jake Mullin has already warned me. You better go get cleaned up then write out your report. I'll want you to hold down this office while I'm away. I'm going to Gadson Flats then on to Jules Crossing. Two of Yaro's gang are on the loose with Yaro's widow, and we could get some trouble from them.'

'I heard tell about it,' Carver said, crushing out the end of his glowing cigar. He got to his feet, and little puffs of dust arose from the folds of his dark, sweat-stained shirt. 'You got some trouble coming to you, Chet. I guess you know that, huh?'

Manning arose, sighing heavily. 'It's unfinished business,' he commented. 'I'll straighten it out. There was certain to be some loose ends left over.'

'You didn't get the chance to clean up completely,' Carver observed. 'Are you fully recovered from your wounds?'

'I'm as fit as I'll ever be,' Manning smiled.

Carver nodded, his keen blue eyes noting there was a stiffness in Manning's manner which would not be concealed by any effort. He had seen it before in men who had survived blood and thunder in the pursuit of duty, and he was aware that Manning was living through a personal crisis.

'I'll go get cleaned up then come back here,' he said, 'Is there anything special I got to watch out for while you're away?'

'Not unless something comes up, and you can wire me at Gadson Flats or Jules Crossing should something break.' Manning dropped a hand to his gunbelt. 'Bolden is away to San Blanca and Aitken should be reporting back from Bedrock Canyon in a day or two.'

'Okay. It's good that everything is quiet.' Carver nodded and departed, and Manning stared after him, his blue eyes reflective, his thoughts slow and heavy.

He left the office and crossed the street to the Blaine house. It was time to eat, and he wanted to talk to Rosa before setting out on his trip. With the spur line to Jules Crossing completed he had no need of a horse, and that prospect pleased him. His wounds were healed but he did not feel up to a jolting saddle unless it became necessary. He thought of Glory Harpe and the two hardcases as he crossed the street. They hated him enough to want to see him dead, and he knew he had to go looking for them. If he tried to ignore their presence he would most likely get a bullet from behind one dark night when he was least expecting it.

'Hi, Chet!' a youthful voice hailed, and Manning glanced around swiftly, breaking stride when he saw Billy Dainton, a young deputy sheriff, coming towards him from the law office. Dainton was only nineteen, a tall youngster, thin, willowy like a sapling, and his pale eyes shone with hero-worship as he confronted Manning. 'If you've got a moment I'd like to talk to you,' he said.

'What's on your mind, Billy? Let's get out of the sun, shall we?'

'I got a report from Gadson Flats that a dead man was found beside the track yesterday,' Dainton said importantly, glancing around the wide, rutted street but not seeing the drab adobe buildings. In his mind's eye he could see a number of masked outlaws running out of the bank carrying bags of stolen money, and himself out there in the midst of them dealing out death coolly and bravely, like Chet Manning had handled the Ben Yaro gang.

'A dead man!' Manning pursed his lips. 'Where was he found, Billy?'

'Some miles north of Gadson Flats. The report said he might have fallen from a train.'

'Did the fall kill him?'

'Nope! He had a single bullet wound in the back. He had been robbed. There was a case with him, opened and the things pulled out. He had no billfold or money on him, and Marshal Loman figures robbery was the motive.'

'And he could have fallen off a train,' Manning mused, 'or been kicked off. Were there tracks around him?'

'Sure! One horse, but the dead man didn't ride it.'

'Okay, Billy. I'm heading up to Gadson Flats shortly. I'll

60

have a chat with Hart Loman.' Manning paused in the shade of the sidewalk. There were beads of sweat on his forehead. 'Be seeing you,' he said, and walked on.

He went to the Blaine house and entered, pausing when he heard female voices, and a frown touched his face when he recognised Netta and Rosa talking together in the parlour. They were discussing him, and he soon gathered that Netta was jealous. He sighed sharply and went quietly to Asa's study, entering without knocking, and the District Superintendent looked up, then leaned back in his seat, mopping his brow.

'Decided what to do yet?' Asa asked.

'Yeah. I'll go north to Gadson Flats. There's something else up there I need to check out. But I got a feeling that Glory and those two outlaws will be holed up in one of the hideouts the badmen use when they're passing through here.'

'Well you know where most of them are situated, but it'll be a long job searching all of them.' Asa scratched his beard.

'I'll make some inspired guesses and check the ones I think may be used. I reckon to pull out tomorrow.'

'Sure thing. Just keep in touch when you can, huh? A wire from any of the stations will reach me.'

'I'll call you to tell you I've nailed those outlaws,' Manning retorted.

'That's the day I'll be waiting for. But there's something else I wanta mention to you, Chet, if you got a minute.'

'Sure. Go ahead. What's on your mind?'

'Netta is acting kind of dreamy. I think she's mooning over you.'

'Well I ain't given her any encouragement, and that kind of entanglement is the last thing I want. I'll stay out of her way, Asa. Anyways, I'll be gone from town for a couple of weeks at least. Don't worry about it.'

Asa sighed heavily and shook his head, and Manning escaped from the office, filled with relief that he had got away so easily.

The next morning he was at the depot awaiting the train going north. It would be a freight, and he figured he could bed down in one of the boxcars to sleep away the time to Gadson Flats. As the train arrived a voice called to him and he turned to see Rosa coming to the station, dressed in the clothes she had worn when they went to end of track. Her figure was beautiful, and Manning caught his breath.

61

'I want to go for a train ride,' she said as he walked towards a boxcar. 'Take me with you, Chet.'

'Heck, I can't do that!' he retorted, pausing to look into her glinting eyes.

'You wouldn't want Uncle Asa to learn that Netta creeps into your bedroom every night, would you?'

Manning caught his breath and clenched his teeth. A sigh escaped him, but he forced a smile, jerking open the door of the boxcar.

'Okay, get in,' he rasped.

He was helping her into the car when a tall, heavily-built man stepped out of another boxcar and paused when he saw them getting into the freight wagon. He was heavy and well muscled, with a fleshy, brooding face and a thin-lipped mouth. Crossed cartridge belts encircled his thick waist and his holsters were tied down.

'Hey!' he yelled. 'Hold on there, mister! Just what do you think you're doing? This aint no passenger train! Get that filly off'n there and stand clear!'

Manning frowned as he continued helping Rosa into the car, but he saw her face take on a shadow of fear as she peered out at the newcomer, who was advancing upon them with purposeful stride. He turned to face the man, not liking the insolent, supercilious expression riding the newcomer's tough features.

'I'm Chet Manning,' he said, and dropped his hand to the butt of his gun. 'What's it to you, mister?'

'Manning?' The man's face changed expression slightly. 'So you're the bossman of the troubleshooters outfit on the railroad! Uhuh! I'm Hank Bolden! I'm one of your new men.'

'Bolden!' Manning nodded. 'I got the word on you. How'd you make out in San Blanca?'

'I'll write out a report. There was a railroad employee name of Johnson who was stealing the freight. I had to plug him before I could arrest him!'

'Old Jed Johnson?'

'That's him!'

'Did you shoot him bad?' Manning demanded.

'Through the shoulder. Another couple of inches and he would have been ready for planting.'

Manning compressed his lips, not liking Bolden's manner or tone. He suppressed a sigh.

'Okay,' he said. 'Report to Joe Carver. He's holding down the office until I get back. I don't know much about you, Bolden, but I'll get around to talking to you when I return. Have you had much experience in this sort of job?'

'I was an agent for the Butterfield Detective Agency operating out of Fort Worth,' Bolden replied, his pale blue eyes steady on Manning's face.

'Why did you quit them?'

'They cramped my style!' Bolden grinned. 'You better get aboard now. You're holding up the train.'

Manning glanced around. The freight was ready to pull out. He sprang into the boxcar and waved a hand to the engineer peering back from the cab. There was an answering toot and the brakeman climbed aboard the caboose at the rear. The train started moving forward and Manning gazed down at Bolden as they departed. Bolden remained staring up at him, grinning insolently, then lifted a hand and waved casually. Manning poked a forefinger at his hatbrim in reply then turned away, moving to where Rosa had seated herself on a crate against a wall of the car.

'Well,' she said in a slightly higher pitched voice than usual. 'I'm sorry I had to use blackmail to get aboard this train, but Netta made a lot of noise last night crossing to your room, and I was on the stairs. I'd been down to the kitchen for a drink of water. There is a lot of truth in those rumours about your reputation after all.'

'I'm a man,' he responded. 'A man is as good as he has to be. I didn't take advantage of Netta. It's what she wanted.'

'That's your business, Chet, and I'm not going to spoil your fun. God knows you need some relaxation, the job you've got. I don't know how you manage to overcome the daily fears. Don't tell me that you don't feel scared sometimes! I know that all you men believe you should not show any emotion. But you are human underneath, all of you, and there are weaknesses in you because you are human. But even the women seem hard. I think Netta and Aunt Polly are wonderful, but they have such a tough attitude towards life.'

'You're a very understanding female,' he commented. 'Your observations are right on the nail. But you have to live out here a long time before you can even begin to understand what makes a westerner tick. It's the tough way of life that coarsens people. The hardcases we can take in our stride. A bullet will stop most of them. But just living in this wilderness does something to a man or a woman.'

'I can see that.' She nodded, glancing through the open doorway at the rough ground flashing by. 'But I hope the surroundings won't affect me like that if I stay for any length of time.'

'What are your plans?' Manning's throat was constricted with unaccustomed emotion. He had to fight an impulse to reach out and touch her. There was nothing sexual in his desire, just an instinctive wish to make contact with someone who was pure and unsullied, uncontaminated by the bad things of life. She was like a clean evening breeze after a long summer day, a refreshing shower of rain after a drought.

'It depends on what my father thinks. But I'd like to stay here. He's the only family I have.'

Manning nodded soberly, aware that he was falling under the spell of her closeness. For the first time in his life he had met a girl whose personality was such that he did not want to drag her immediately into bed and make love to her. Netta was perfect for sex, and it seemed right for him to assail her at every opportunity, but Rosa made him aware that a woman had more than one use in life. He sighed heavily, hardly able to understand what was happening to him, but he was content merely to be in her company, and settled down to some serious thinking about the situation. He could not permit her presence to distract him from his grim task.

They were ready to detrain when they reached Gadson Flats, and he paused at the telegraph office to ask for messages. There were none and he led Rosa out to the street of the little railroad town, pausing when he saw Hart Lowman, the town marshal, coming towards them. A grin of welcome touched his lips.

'Hart, I was about to call on you!' he exclaimed.

'Chet! I got word that you were back and figured it wouldn't be too long before you showed up.' Loman was tall and beefy, with narrowed brown eyes that took in Rosa without appearing to do so. The law star on his shirt front glinted in the sunlight. 'I'm glad you got over your wounds. You did a great job with Yaro's bunch. But there are still some of that gang on the loose, I hear.'

'We'll talk later,' Manning replied. 'This is Ike Mozee's daughter Rosa. I'll see her to the hotel to wait for the train to Jules Crossing, then I'll come to your office for a yarn.'

'Miss Mozee!' Loman lifted his hat graciously, his eyes shining. 'I'm pleased to make your acquaintance. I know your father well! He is a good railroad man!'

'Hello, marshal!' she responded.

'I'll be in my office waiting for you, Chet,' Loman said and touched his hat to Rosa as he went on his way.

Manning secured a room for her in the hotel then went back to the street, and although it was late afternoon there was no relaxation of the day's heat. He was sweating as he started towards the law office.

The wide street was practically deserted. There were a couple of saddle horses standing at a hitchrail outside a saloon, and a buckboard was being loaded in front of the general store. Nowhere was there much activity, until Hart Loman suddenly appeared in the doorway of his office, followed by another man. Loman paused, pulling his gun, then started across the street, running away from Manning, making for the bank, and Manning felt a swift pang stab him as he caught a glimpse of three horses standing at rails around the bank. There was other movement there too. A man was standing in the doorway of the bank, looking casual, but there was a pistol in his hand.

Manning caught his breath and began running forward. The bank was being robbed! In an instant his mental turmoil was gone, thrust into the background by his instincts and training. He drew his gun without being aware of the action, and as he did so Hart Loman began to shoot, shattering the brooding silence with the raucous crash of his Colt's thunder.

Manning flinched but did not check his stride. It was the unwritten duty of all honest men to go to the aid of a peace officer and he had never shirked his duty. He saw a bunch of men appearing from the bank, and they began to return fire, their guns smoking. He ran as fast as he could towards the scene, and horror rippled through him, for just ahead Hart Loman was going down in the dust!

Chapter Six

Manning cut loose with his pistol as soon as he was within effective range of the bank, but by that time the robbers had mounted and were spurring away along the street, exchanging shots with the one or two men who dared take them on from doorways and other cover. He saw Trig Forbes ducking into the alley, recognising the big man. His lips pulled tight as he tried to wing Forbes, but the outlaw disappeared from sight. By the time Manning reached the alley mouth, Forbes had mounted and was gone.

Reloading, Manning went back to where Loman was stretched out, and already a townsman was bent over the inert marshal. The man looked up when Manning approached and slowly shook his head. Shock flooded Manning and he halted in midstride, staring down at the dead lawman.

A crowd quickly gathered while Manning stood motionless, listening to the angry, shocked voices. No one seemed to know what to do and everyone was shouting at once. Manning called for order, and when silence came he spoke sharply.

'Those robbers are getting away while you're arguing here,' he said. 'Grab your horses and take out after them.'

There was a rush towards the stable, but some of the men made no attempt to leave. They stood in small groups, looking at the dead lawman and staring at the bank. Two men came out of the bank, one ashen faced and trembling, and he was talking rapidly in a high-pitched voice to the other. They halted and stared down at the dead Hart Loman, and Manning yelled for someone to fetch a blanket. He went to the two men from the bank.

'Did you recognise any of the robbers?' he demanded.

'One of them was Trig Forbes, from Ben Yaro's old gang,' the teller replied. 'I recognised him plain enough. It didn't take him long to get some new hardcases around him.'

'I recognised him myself,' Manning said. 'Any idea who was with him?'

The teller shook his head. He was badly shocked.

'Do you know Grat Trimble from Buffalo Junction?' Manning demanded. 'He ran a freighting business but was an undercover man for Yaro.'

'Sure. Know him well!' the teller nodded, 'What about him?'

'Was he one of the others?'

'I couldn't say. There was one man outside on the sidewalk. I didn't get a good look at him, but the other two inside the bank with Forbes were strangers to me. Looks like you've made the railroad too hot for them outlaws so they're coming back to bank-robbing.'

'Could it have been a woman waiting outside with the horses?' Manning persisted.

'I don't think so!' The teller shook his head. 'I figure he was too tall for a woman.'

Manning nodded and turned away. Someone was draping a blanket over the dead marshal and, as he went back to the hotel, Manning tried to shake off his own sense of shock. Hart Loman was dead! It had happened in the space of a split second, and it could happen to anyone who lived dangerously. He wondered if he were losing his nerve and fought against the panic which tried to fill his mind. He was all right! He assured himself fiercely. He had not hung back when the shooting started. He had run into it, using his own gun. He frowned as he entered the hotel, and Rosa was there in the lobby, looking pale, listening to the rumours that were flying. She ran to Manning when she saw him, and almost threw herself into his arms.

'I heard you were involved!' she said vibrantly. 'Someone even said you'd been shot down.'

'Not me,' he retorted harshly. 'It was the marshal.'

'Mr Loman?' she asked in horror, and he nodded. 'But you were on your way to talk to him!' She seemed to cringe, and Manning put a hand under her elbow.

'That's the way it goes,' he said harshly. 'You never know when your time has come! Perhaps it's the best way at that!' He sounded cynical, and she looked quickly into his face, searching for emotion, but his features were expressionless, his blue eyes blazing, and she eased back from him, a little

67

embarrassed by the way she had shown her concern.

'What will happen now?' she demanded.

'The town will elect a new marshal and they'll forget all about Hart Loman in a couple of weeks. But I saw the robbers, and one of them was an outlaw who was arrested when Yaro's gang was wiped out. He was one of the gang; the only active member to survive.'

'And you want him?' she questioned.

'Yes. He has acted against the railroad.' He shook his head slowly. 'I'll go after him.'

She sighed, her face taut and pale. Manning patted her shoulder.

'Why don't you go up and rest until it's time for us to catch the train?' he suggested.

'I don't think I could rest,' she replied, shaking her head. 'Now I can understand why my mother left father all those years ago. No woman should be forced to endure the endless torture of wondering if her man will die or not! I always blamed her, deep inside, for running away from father, but not any more. I didn't understand then. But I do now!'

He drew a long breath and held it for a moment, his eyes filled with shadow.

'Would you rather go back to Buffalo Junction?' he asked softly. 'If you're not used to this country then you might be better off leaving it altogether. Most of this territory is still untamed, and until the badmen have been taken it won't alter. It's not fit for women and children to live in!'

'You have business in Jules Crossing, don't you? I don't want to put you to any extra trouble. I'll travel with you to Jules Crossing and you can take me home afterwards.'

'We've got a couple of hours to wait before the train leaves. If you'll stay here I'll see what can be done in town, and I have a couple of wires to send. With a new gang loose in the area the railroad will need to be on its toes.'

She nodded and he departed once more, making his way to the station. He sent a wire to Buffalo Junction informing Asa Blaine of the bank robbery and naming Trig Forbes as one of the robbers, and asking for a troubleshooter to be sent to the town. Then he went to the law office to find the mayor there with a number of other leading men of the town.

'We need a replacement, Chet,' Mayor Newark said when

Manning entered the office. 'Hart Loman was a good man and we didn't even need a deputy marshal with him around. But there's no one handy to step into his boots. Do you know anyone who could take over?'

Manning shook his head.

'Can you run a posse to get after those robbers?' the mayor persisted.

'I'm sorry,' Manning said. 'I'm on railroad business right now. I've got to go to Jules Crossing. I'm catching the next train through. I want Trig Forbes myself, but I have to go to Jules Crossing before I can take out after him.'

'Pity you wasn't a lawman, Chet,' Newark retorted. 'We could do with you around.'

'I can't be in two places at once,' Manning replied. 'I wish I could help out. But my job keeps me real busy.'

He left them wrangling about the dead marshal's successor and went along the street to the undertaker's. Mort Downey was a tall, thin man of sixty, with long, discoloured grey whiskers and pale blue eyes.

'Howdy, Chet!' he greeted. 'Heard you was gonna show up to take a look at the dead man I picked up from beside the railroad track. I got him out back, and I need to get him planted pronto. He's beginning to stink the place out.'

'Okay, let's get it over with!' Manning said, drawing a swift breath.

Downey nodded and turned to lead the way through to the back of his place. Manning tightened his lips at the dreadful smell which pervaded the hot atmosphere, and his eyes narrowed when he saw Hart Loman's body stretched out on a table. Downey had been in the process of stripping the dead marshal, and Manning clenched his teeth as he followed the undertaker across to a blanket-covered figure at the back of the long room.

One glance at the dead gambler was sufficient for Manning to identify him, and he turned away, trying to hold his breath, sickened by the cloying stench. He did not breathe again until they reached the front shop, and did not pause there but hurried out to the sidewalk, exhaling sharply before filling his lungs with fresh air. Downey followed him, grinning tightly.

'It gets you, huh?' the undertaker demanded. 'It's the hot weather. But did you recognise him?'

'Yeah, for what it's worth.' Manning spoke shakily. He felt sick deep inside. His mouth was dry and his lips seemed to stick together. 'I kicked him off the train about eight miles north of here.'

'That's about where I picked him up,' Downey agreed. 'Why did you kick him off the train?'

'Gambling and cheating! But how in hell did he come to get himself shot in that exact spot? He was shot in the back, wasn't he?'

'That's right. But he wasn't on railroad property at the time so it ain't your worry. Now Loman is dead I reckon Sheriff Barnes will have to send a deputy in here to take over. There ain't anyone else around who can hold down the town marshal's job.'

'Very likely,' Manning said. 'I sent a wire to my office in Buffalo Junction, so word of what happened here will get to Barnes. He may even come out here himself!'

'That'll be the day.' Downey snickered as he turned away. 'The only times Barnes leaves the county seat is when it's time to go electioneering.'

Manning walked away, still suffering from nausea, and he went along to the saloon for whisky. There was a crowd of men inside, all talking about the robbery and Hart Loman's death, but Manning wanted no part of it. He drank three fingers of whisky and departed swiftly, feeling stronger inside as he went back to the hotel.

He dropped a hand to his gunbutt, trying to steady his mind. Before the Yaro gang clean-up he had killed seven men for the railroad and it had not bothered him at all. Then came the showdown with Yaro's bunch and he had pushed up his tally of killings in a few days. That was what caused his uncertainty, he knew, and guessed he just had to wait for his mind to accept the grim facts.

By the time he collected Rosa and they went to the depot for the train to Jules Crossing he was feeling more settled, and they took their seats and chatted. But Manning was still on edge, and he stared out at the countryside, knowing almost every feature on the trip to the end of the eastern spur. He pointed out the landmarks to Rosa and kept the girl occupied. Evening drew on and it was dark when they alighted from the train, to be greeted by Barney McCall, the town marshal. After greeting Manning he accompanied them to the hotel. Manning badly needed to talk with McCall and, after ensuring Rosa was comfortable in a room, he went down to the bar with the town marshal.

The big lawman looked troubled as he bought Manning a beer. There was a crowd in the bar and their voices merged into a heavy buzz of sound. Manning shook his head, emptying his glass and motioning for the marshal to accompany him outside. They stood on the sidewalk in the shadows, a cool breeze blowing gently into their faces.

'Barney, what can you tell me about outlaws in these parts?' Manning demanded. 'You had any trouble around here?'

'No.' McCall shook his head. 'You busted Squint Delmont's gang, then took care of Yaro and his bunch. I figure you've scared all the other badhats out of the territory.'

'You heard about the robbery earlier in Gadson Flats?'

'It came over the telegraph.' McCall sighed heavily. 'That kind of news travels fast. You saw Trig Forbes among the four robbers, huh?'

'I recognised him!' Manning's voice was low and harsh. 'I figure I'm gonna have to go out and look for him, Barney! And Yaro's widow. I figure they're trying to scrape together a new gang.'

'Looks like they've succeeded. And now Hart Loman is dead the price on Forbes's head will go up. I reckon there won't be many out to pick up that bounty, Chet.'

'I want him!' There was a grim note in Manning's voice. 'But Trimble and Glory Harpe are out to get me. I'm having to watch my back now. I've got to find out if they parted from Forbes after she busted him out of jail.'

'Why would she bust him out if it wasn't to get him to work with her?' McCall demanded. 'And if she wanted him to get you then why was he robbing the bank in Gadson Flats?'

'Neither Glory nor Trimble were with the robbers today,' Manning mused.

'You're gonna have to pick them up!' McCall shook his head. He could barely see Manning's face in the light coming from the hotel windows. Stars were glittering in the velvet sky. The night was pleasant after the long hours of glaring sunlight that had tortured the land. 'If I hear anything at all about those three I'll get word to you, Chet. But, like I said, I reckon you'll have to go out and hunt them down to make sure of them. If you leave it they'll show up on your tail when you're least expecting it, and you won't get an even break. On top of that, you've got to see S & W are first to reach Apache Pass. Western Pacific won't give up now.'

'That's what I'm afraid of.' Manning nodded slowly, and there was a lump in his throat. 'My next stop is end of track and the construction camp. I've got to get things organised for the last push to Apache Pass. From what I've heard we're ahead of Western Pacific and I want it to stay like that. But everything will have to be done the hard way, I figure. When I get Rosa back to Buffalo Junction I'll take a couple of my new men and set out on a hunt. Forbes might be hard to find, but if Trimble and Glory Harpe are still around then I ought to be able to catch them.'

'Things should be pretty quiet around the railroad now Yaro and his gang are done for,' McCall remarked, and they chatted for some time about the past.

But Manning was impatient, and when he took his leave of McCall and went back into the hotel to take Rosa to supper he found himself wondering about the girl. She had captivated him in the few days he had known her. He had never seen a prettier girl, and none had attracted him so much. He had fancied himself in love with more than one girl in the years since his youth, but he had never been serious. Now he could feel a powerful emotion taking him over, invading his entire consciousness, ousting his more normal thoughts of duty, and there was an ache in his heart that made him want to be with her. He was discovering that when he was not in Rosa's company he felt depressed and restless, and the thought of seeing the girl again made him forget everything but that desire.

They had supper together, and Rosa talked about her life. Manning was content merely to watch her, and he dared not ask about her plans for the future. He studied her fine features and saw the lanternlight glinting in her dark eyes.

Before they could leave the dining-room Barney McCall appeared, his large face intent, his lips tight, and he threaded his way between the tables and paused at Manning's side, apologising for interrupting their meal.

'There's something I'd like to talk over with you, Chet, and it won't wait,' the town marshal said. 'If you wouldn't mind stepping outside for a moment.'

Manning caught his breath, for he knew McCall would not bother him unless it was urgent, and he hastily excused himself and followed the marshal to the door. When they reached the lobby, McCall spoke tersely.

'I've been making a round of the town, Chet, and just now, as I was passing Trimble's freight office, I fancied I heard someone inside. The office and house have been locked up ever since Trimble was arrested. But it's likely he's sneaked in here to collect some of his gear. I wouldn't go in on my own in case it is Trimble and he's not alone. I figured, before I fetched a couple of dependable men, that you would want to be in on this.'

'You bet!' Manning spoke without hesitation, but a pang stabbed through him as he dropped his hand to the butt of his gun. He had been telling himself ever since the showdown with Yaro's gang that he had not lost his nerve, and he believed it. But now was the moment of truth. He would find out the hard way if he had turned yellow! He clenched his teeth, glancing back into the dining-room, taking in the picture of Rosa sitting at the table waiting for him, and it seemed that she was in another world. 'Let's go,' he said harshly. 'The sooner we get it done the better.'

'Just the two of us?' McCall demanded.

'No sense rousing out the whole town for what might be nothing at all,' Manning retorted, and saw McCall grin.

'I'd take on a dozen badmen with you at my side, Chet,' the marshal said tightly.

They walked along the street, and Manning felt as if he were entering a nightmare. He shivered and sweat dripped down his face. His hands were trembling, and he could only wonder what was happening to him. He had been shot before, more than once, and after each occasion he had found his nerve strong and steady. He had come out on top after the Yaro showdown, but now he was weak inside, nervous and uncertain, like a green kid out on his first tough chore.

When they reached the house beside the big, shadowed freight yard, McCall drew his gun. Starlight glinted on the bared metal. Manning dropped his hand to his gunbutt but did not pull the weapon. They remained motionless, listening and watching, and Manning could hear the blood pounding in his temples and was afraid McCall might overhear it. He tightened

73

his lips and narrowed his eyes. If shooting began he would go into it like a man, notwithstanding his feelings. He would not mar his reputation.

'Sounds quiet now,' McCall observed in an undertone. 'But I didn't imagine it, Manning.' He paused, then went on. 'I guess I am a little jumpy after what happened in Gadson Flats today, but that's natural, I guess, although I wouldn't admit that to anyone but you. I reckon you understand a man's feelings after he's risked his life day after day for a long period.'

'Only too well!' Manning retorted, shaking his head. 'I'm nervous as a kitten right now, Barney, and I wouldn't admit that to anyone else. But standing here won't check out this place. Let's go in. We'll try to cover one another.'

'I'm the local lawman,' McCall replied harshly. 'I better go first.'

'No!' Manning reached out and gripped the marshal's arm. 'I want to do this, Barney. You cover me! If Trimble is in there then he's my man and I want to take him.'

'You've talked me out of it!' McCall chuckled harshly. 'I'll be right behind you and ready to cover. If there is shooting and you get the chance, drop flat so I can buy into it.'

'Don't you worry,' Manning replied. 'I'll be practically on my knees before I get in there.'

He grinned, trying to relieve the terrible pressure that had built up inside to constrict his throat and chest, and he drew his gun, moving forward to the door. He found the door locked and began a circuit of the building, pausing to check each window he came to. He was trembling inside, but whether from antici- pation or fear he did not know. Then he found a window that was open, and coldness filled him although he sweated freely. He turned and motioned to McCall, a shapeless figure at his back, and McCall's pale blur of a face pressed closer, the marshal's teeth glinting in the shadows.

'I'm going in!' Manning said in an undertone. 'You better stay outside in case anything breaks. One man in there alone is all that's needed to check the place out.'

'You're on your own!' McCall retorted flatly. 'But be careful, Chet!'

There was a strange eagerness in Manning's mind as he heaved himself upon the window sill, trying desperately to remain silent, and he was breathing heavily as he dropped

74

lightly over the sill into the darkness beyond. His pulses were racing and every nerve in his body was tense. He paused, listening intently, but heard nothing to arouse his suspicions. He told himself that it need not be Trimble in here. A local badman might have yielded to the temptation to check out an empty house. But he stiffened as he became aware of a smell of cigar smoke drifting slowly through the black atmosphere, no doubt activated by the open window, for the house had been closed since Trimble's arrest weeks before. He exhaled slowly, extending his left hand, feeling his way around the unfamiliar room, unable to avoid making slight sounds as he moved, and he fought down the frightening pictures being conjured up by his hardworking imagination. He was at a disadvantage making all the moves, and it bothered him, not because of the disadvantage but because he was worried about it.

Then he came up against a desk, and his slowly moving left hand touched an ash tray upon its invisible surface. He winced as his probing fingers found the butt of a cigar, for it was still hot, and then he knew for certain that he was not alone in the room. He eased down on one knee, tightening his grip upon his gun, covering himself with the desk. He swallowed the knot of tension in his throat and drew a sharp breath.

'Okay, whoever you are!' he suddenly snapped, his tones echoing. 'I know you're in the room! You can't get away. There's someone covering me outside. Throw down your gun and climb out through that window!'

His tones had barely died away before a gun blasted overwhelmingly, its reddish-orange flash lighting up the inner doorway with ruddy flame, revealing a figure standing there, and three shots split and tattered the darkness, the bullets crashing into the desk as the man aimed in the direction of Manning's voice. Splinters flew out of the desktop, some of them striking Manning's face. The second tugged at his hatbrim. A terrific punch struck his left arm below the shoulder as the third shot blasted, and he went down flat, triggering his Colt in swift reply, his lips pulled back, his teeth bared, a fierce exultation bursting like a savage blossom in his mind. He emptied his gun at the doorway, firing more than bullets as he swept into action. He was ridding himself of doubt and indecision! His nerve had not broken. He was still as ready to fight as he had always been!

Chapter Seven

Both Trimble and Glory found time heavy upon their hands as they sat around the hideout awaiting Trig Forbes's return. They spent long periods discussing what they would do to Chet Manning when they finally caught him, but even that diversion palled as the days passed in an endless round of heat-stricken lounging within the close confines of the hideout. Trimble was the first to crack, and he awakened one morning and refused to eat Glory's cooking. When she challenged him he cursed and shook his head impatiently.

'What the hell are we doing around here like a couple of three-legged mules trapped in a box canyon?' he demanded. 'We don't need to get mixed up with criminals. That can only lead to bad trouble. We could be out there doing something about the situation. Chet Manning is back, and as like as not he's been moving around the area. All we've got to do is drop on to him and take him prisoner. This sitting around is playing hell with my nerves and patience. I want to get it over with and get the hell out of here.'

'Trig came up with a pretty good idea,' Glory protested. 'I figure the railroad owes us both a living, Grat! We won't get it if we don't stick around. If Trig can find those other men he's gone after then we should see things begin to happen.'

'We'll do that okay!' Trimble snapped, his face brooding, his dark eyes showing a troubled expression. 'I don't trust Forbes! He's a real badman! And if you could see the way he's been looking at you sometimes you'd be real worried about it!'

'If you weren't old enough to be my father I'd say you were jealous, Grat!' she retorted, but her expression showed that she was perturbed by his words. She suppressed a shudder, thinking of the affair she'd had with Forbes. It had been at the request of her husband because Yaro had feared that Forbes's restlessness

76

would result in a mutiny by the gang. She spoke in a lower tone. 'To tell you the truth, I don't feel easy when Trig is around. He gives me the creeps! But we need him! We've got to live while we're waiting to get Manning!'

'He won't give us much!' Trimble said tightly. 'He don't even appreciate the fact that you busted him out of jail. He took five hundred dollars off that gambler, but we didn't see any of the dough. I told you I got money in several towns.'

'Forget it! You couldn't get it out of the bank!' Glory sneered.

'I got some in my office in Jules Crossing.' He spoke swiftly, suddenly remembering the money in the house.

'How much?'

'About a thousand dollars!' He sounded hopeful. 'It should be enough for us. Our needs are small right now.'

'But we've got to think of later, after Manning is dead!' Glory scowled. 'The railroad owes us something, Grat! It took away your living, and when Manning killed Yaro he did me out of my way of life!'

'We could take a train ourselves!' Trimble said softly.

'Just the two of us?' She shook her head. 'Trig knows all about that business and he figured to need three more men at least.'

'I don't reckon I'm cut out to be a train robber in that sense,' he retorted angrily. 'We could wreck a train. If we loosened a couple of rails at the foot of a down grade we'd have the train over on its side and all smashed up, and we could loot it in our own time!'

'Picking through the wreckage like a couple of buzzards!' she retorted, her voice quivering with disgust. 'What do you take me for? Sure I'm mad as hell at Chet Manning! I'd do anything to see him dead! But I won't involve innocent people in my troubles. It's Manning I want and I'll get him alone and finish him.'

'That's where we fall out then!' Trimble spoke harshly. 'I want to see Manning dead, by God, after the way he treated me! But I won't be happy until I've caused the railroad plenty of trouble. I'll make the S & W sorry they ever put tracks through here.'

Glory stared at his taut face for a moment, seeing the naked hatred in his dark eyes, and sighed heavily.

'Grat, we both want the same thing really, so we better not fall out over this. Maybe you're right about Trig and the others. Perhaps we don't need them. Trig might not even come back here now. Do you think we could make out if we rode alone?'

'We can try it,' he said eagerly. 'I ain't liked this set-up from the moment you busted me and Forbes out of jail. Let's get out of here and handle our own business ourselves. I feel a lot happier knowing we won't have Forbes around.'

She nodded slowly, although her face expressed doubt. But she agreed and they went to prepare to leave. While Glory sacked some provisions and filled their canteens, Trimble saddled their mounts, and he was in a fever of apprehension until they had departed and ridden clear of the hideout. He feared Trig Forbes, and suspected that the big outlaw had merely fallen in with their plans because it suited his own purpose to have them around.

They rode all day, and the more miles they put between themselves and the hideout the easier Trimble felt. He knew the country intimately and headed for Jules Crossing. But they camped that night and slept rough, ready to go on next day, and reached Jules Crossing just before nightfall, exhausted and dusty, and lay up in cover on the outskirts until full darkness came.

'Grat, will there be anyone watching your house, do you think?' Glory demanded as shadows crawled about them.

'Not after all this time. They closed the freight line after I was arrested. What's on your mind?'

'I could do with cleaning up! I need a bath and some clothes that are fit to wear.'

'It might be too risky.' He was concerned about coming back. Everyone knew him and he was on edge because if things went wrong and he had to start shooting he might be forced to kill people he knew and liked. 'All I want to do is get in there, grab my dough and pull out. There are some clothes in the house that belonged to my wife and daughter. I'll bring some out to you. I could do with a change of clothes myself. But we don't have time to clean up, Glory. And I want to go in there alone. You better stick around here with the horses. I won't be long. Then when we got the money we can pull out and make for Buffalo Junction. Once we get on Manning's trail we can make our plans to take him!'

She nodded, suppressing a sigh. Although she had travelled the rough country with Ben Yaro she had kept clean, and the fact that she was living rough now made her depressed and gave her a sense of remoteness which added to the shock and grief she was suffering. But her emotions had twisted, and hatred for Chet Manning had diverted all other feelings into a desire for revenge. She knew that nothing but the death of the man she hated would assuage those bitter feelings.

'I'll wait with the horses,' she said softly. 'When Manning is dead we can move on and become people again.'

'I figure I can move now,' he cut in. 'It's dark enough to cover me. You stay put here, in case I have to leave in a hurry and need my horse.'

'Don't forget a change of clothes for me!' she called as he slipped away into the gloom.

Trimble sighed with relief as he moved forward on his own. He felt a burden slip from his shoulders. Being in Glory's company, and sensing her brooding hatred, affected him only slightly, but the fact that she was female had added to his mental problems. His wife had died early in their marriage and his daughter, about Glory's age, had run away with a visiting drummer years before. Bitterness lived permanently in Grat Trimble's heart, and he had sought to cover his loneliness over the years by throwing all his energies into his freight line while working under cover for Yaro. But now he was on the run and the future seemed bleak and uncertain.

He reached the shadows surrounding his house and crouched silently in cover, his thin lips twisted by bitter thoughts. He dropped a hand to the butt of his gun as a sound alerted him and peered around like a cornered mountain cat until he was satisfied that there was no one near.

Knowing the house intimately, he made for his study window, remembering that the window catch was faulty, and within seconds he had the window open and was climbing inside. He left the window open while he stood listening intently, wondering if the law had set a man to watch the place, but as the long moments passed and there were no suspicious sounds he accepted that there was no danger, and moved confidently to his desk. He dared not light a lamp, but he knew this room only too well and did not need to see. He discovered that the chair was not behind the desk where it usually stood, and dropped to one knee, his hands reaching out carefully. His left hand encountered the whisky bottle which was normally kept on the desk and he uncorked it, tilting the bottle to his eager lips. He had been longing for a strong drink for many days.

The bottle was empty when he lowered it, and a warm feeling spread through him as he set it down. He lit a cigar as he moved to his safe on the left of the desk, and fetched the spare key, which was under a loose floorboard near the safe. His hands trembled as he unlocked the heavy door and swung it open. But his elation fled when he searched with his hands and discovered that the sheaf of paper money he kept in the safe was not there. At first he could not accept the fact, and dragged out ledgers and other papers in a blind panic. But the money was gone! He finally sat back on his heels and stared into the shadows.

Had he been robbed? The thought crossed his mind but he immediately discarded it. The safe had not been broken open! Then he drew a sharp breath and held it for long, pulsating moments. All his belongings had been taken from him when he had been arrested, and his bunch of keys had been amongst them. The lawmen must have come to the house and used them. Perhaps they had removed the money for fear that he might sneak into town one dark night and collect it.

Disillusionment flooded him and he got to his feet, breathing hard. He stubbed out the cigar as he moved around the desk, and almost fell over the chair that had been moved from behind it. He kicked the chair viciously, sending it crashing over, then froze, scared by what he had done. As the echoes died away he listened intently. A heavy silence encompassed the house, and he was afraid that a passer-by might have overheard him.

He was about to leave when he recalled Glory's request for clothes, and a sigh escaped him as he left the office and made his way up the stairs to the bedroom his daughter had used. He searched in the dark for a couple of dresses and a shirt and pair of pants, then collected underclothes from a drawer. By the time he was ready to leave, both arms were heavily laden, and he descended the stairs and re-entered the study, pausing in midstride as he crossed the threshold. His alert senses warned that someone was climbing through the window. He caught a glimpse of a dark figure silhouetted against the night and moved back instantly, wondering if it were Glory. But he discounted that idea immediately and emptied his right arm, crushing the clothes into a tight bundle under his left arm and reaching for his gun as he did so.

He remained motionless, silent and deadly, until Chet Manning's tones cut through the darkness. A coldness swept over him then, and he listened intently to the sharp words warning him that he was trapped.

An unreasonable fury exploded in Trimble's mind as he recognised Manning's voice, and before he was aware of it his trigger finger jerked convulsively. He fired three shots, filling the study with smoke and flame, driving out the silence with the blustering reports, and he stepped back immediately, turning instinctively to run. As he moved there was answering fire from the room, and he heard bullets splintering into the door as he moved. Now he was scared, and hurried through the darkness of the ground floor kitchen, jerking out the bar and dragging open the door. He panted as he ran clear, his muscles tensed in anticipation of a bullet. His ears were bemused by the heavy sounds of shooting that had erupted inside the house. But there was no further shooting and he crossed the back lots and lost himself in the shadow of his own barn. He heard a horse stamping inside but did not pause. He kept moving until he was in the clear.

By the time he reached the outskirts of town, Trimble was in a more composed state, and he still clutched the clothes he had brought for Glory as he made his way to the spot where she waited with their horses. She challenged him from the shadows and he answered quickly. The next moment they were together, and the woman was in a high state of alarm.

'What was that shooting?' she demanded harshly.

He explained in trembling tones, his hatred rising again as he mentioned Chet Manning, and Glory fell silent, clenching her hands and biting her lip. She dared not ask the question that forced itself into her mind, but she had to know the worst.

'Did you hit Manning?' she demanded. 'Is he dead?'

'I don't know!' Trimble shook his head. His teeth were chattering now as reaction set in. He was not a coward, but he was only too well aware of the type of man Chet Manning was, and he did not relish the risk. He would have shot Manning in the back from cover, but not even his hatred of the man would move him to walk into the open to exchange shots with the railroad troubleshooter. Manning was too fast and too good for any ordinary man to face.

'We can't ride out until we're certain he's dead!' Glory told him in steady tones.

'I'm not sticking around,' he replied, shaking his head. He thrust the pile of clothes into her arms. 'These are what you asked for. Now we'd better make tracks out of here.'

'Did you get your money?'

'No.' He spoke through clenched teeth. 'It was gone from the safe. I reckon it was taken out and put into the bank for safe keeping. Perhaps they figured that I might sneak back for it.'

'But we can't do anything without money!'

'I know, and I'm thinking about it!' He shook his head. 'I don't reckon we've got a chance now. The town will be in an uproar because of the shooting. We'd better get out of here. They'll know it was me sneaking around the house and a posse will come out looking.'

'I'm not leaving until I know what's happened to Manning,' Glory said resolutely. 'If he is dead then we'll be wasting our time and risking our lives by sticking around.'

'Money is more important than getting him,' Trimble argued.

'But you can't get any!' she countered.

'I can try Howard Belling!'

'The bank is closed!'

'I can go to his house. I went to supper with Belling a number of times. We were close friends.'

'You go talk to Belling while I look around town and try to find out what happened to Manning. Get some money if you can, Grat. The only alternative is to go back to Trig Forbes!'

Trimble suppressed a shiver and nodded grimly.

'I'll go see Belling. But you watch out what you're doing, Glory. If you're picked up it will be the end of you. No one will get the chance to break open the jail again.'

'They won't take me,' she said harshly, a hand on the gun buckled around her slender waist. 'The horses will be okay here. I'll meet you back at this spot in about an hour.'

Trimble nodded and they walked together until they reached the outskirts of town. Then they parted, and Trimble stared after her until she disappeared into the shadows. He shook his head slowly as he considered, and then went on his way, reaching the back of the banker's house without incident, although there were a number of men around the street, disturbed by the shooting.

Trimble fumbled his way through the shadows to a lighted window, and risked a glance inside. He saw Belling's house-keeper in the kitchen, preparing supper, and moved on, making for the front of the house. There was a lighted window in Belling's study, but the curtains were drawn, preventing him getting a view of the interior. He pinched his lips together in worried indecision. Was the banker alone?

Knowing that time was wasting, Trimble went to the front door and tried it, drawing a swift breath when it opened to his touch. He entered the house, his hand upon the butt of his gun. He crossed to the door of Belling's study and opened it, entering the room quietly, ready to pull his holstered weapon. But Belling was alone, busy on some papers before him at the desk. He was not aware of Trimble's presence until the door made a sound as Trimble closed it. Then Belling looked up, his face changing expression slightly as he recognised his visitor.

'Grat!' Belling got to his feet, a tall, portly man with glinting white hair. His pale grey eyes were narrowed as he stared at Trimble's dusty figure. 'What are you doing in town? You must know that the law is looking for you.'

'I know!' There was a harsh note in Trimble's voice which betrayed his desperation. 'I need some money, Howard. I've just looked in my safe in the house and found my dough there is missing.'

'It's in the bank. Marshal McCall paid it in. There was just over a thousand dollars, if I remember correctly.'

'That's about right,' Trimble agreed. 'You must have some cash in the house, Howard. Pay me out now and make it right with yourself in the morning.'

'I can't do that, Grat, and you know it.' Belling spoke firmly. 'I have no power to withdraw any money from your account. In any case, the law has frozen your account. Your money is impounded pending the court hearing against you. The railroad may be suing for damages and, if they win their case, your account will be used to pay your costs.'

'The hell it will!' There was a tight, angry note in Trimble's voice, and he half-drew his pistol. 'You better accept that I'm desperate, Howard, and advance me some money. Tell the law about it by all means, and state that I used a gun to get what I wanted. But you have a pile of dough in your bank belonging to me and I want some of it.'

'I don't have any money here in the house,' Belling said in a smooth voice. 'And I can't go down to the bank at this time of night. The law will probably be on the watch for you, and you must have taken quite a chance to come here tonight.'

'I'm not leaving empty-handed, Howard.' Trimble jerked his gun out of its holster and levelled it at the banker. 'I can tell by your manner and your words that you're no longer a friend of mine. Okay! My life has been ruined and I know it. But I've banked with you close on twenty years and there's a big pile of my dough now, sitting in your safes. You're not gonna turn me away empty-handed, Howard. I want some dough and you are gonna give it to me. I'll sign a receipt if that will make you any happier. Now don't give me any trouble! Just give me the money. My life is in jeopardy and I know it. So I ain't likely to let you forget it for a moment. Now come on. Quit stalling! Open your safe and pay me out.'

Belling shook his head, realising that it was useless trying to reason with Trimble, and opened the right-hand drawer in the desk and took out a bunch of keys. Getting to his feet, he crossed to the big safe standing in a corner and unlocked it. Trimble watched him, gun ready, and his dark eyes glittered as Belling produced a wad of bills. The transaction was made in silence, and Trimble signed a receipt for the money. He grinned with relief as he pocketed the cash, then moved towards the door.

'That's better,' he commented. 'Now don't make a mistake, Howard, and call for help until I've been gone some time, will you? I don't want to have to kill anyone, but I will if I have to.'

'I'll report to the marshal in twenty minutes,' Belling said. 'That's all I can promise you, Grat.'

'That's enough!' Trimble departed, letting himself out of the house and hurrying back to where he had left Glory. He moved steadily, watching his surroundings, and now his feelings had changed completely. He had money and that spelled success. Nothing else mattered. His confidence returned and he believed they would even get Chet Manning now!

He reached the horses and turned to look for Glory, catching a glimpse of a shadowy figure coming towards him from behind the animals.

'Glory!' he called hoarsely. 'Is that you?'

'Hard luck, Trimble!' a sharp voice replied. 'Stand still! I've got you in view and my gun is covering you. Get your hands up!'

Trimble almost choked with shock, and a terrible frustration boiled inside him, but he could do nothing but surrender, and raised his hands slowly in mute despair.

Chapter Eight

Manning clutched his arm as he staggered to his feet, his ears ringing from the sound of the shooting, and he paused and groped for his gun, which had fallen to the desk. He snatched up the weapon and reloaded, trying to listen for sounds in the house other than the dying echoes of the shots. McCall was at the open window, urgently calling his name, and he replied, informing the marshal of the situation.

'Stay where you are and I'll check the back of the house,' McCall yelled.

Manning held his gun, his left arm at his side, and recognised the familiar numb sensation in the limb. When the numbness wore off there would be pain, and he trembled inside as he considered that he still carried wounds that were not completely healed. It was an example of what his life had become, and he gritted his teeth as he waited for McCall to return.

Presently the town marshal's voice echoed through the house, calling his name, and Manning left the room to find McCall standing by the back door. His ears were still ringing from the shooting as he stared at the lawman.

'This door was open when I got here, Chet, and there was no sign of anyone running away,' McCall said. 'Did you get any idea who it was?'

'None! I called a challenge and he started shooting.' Manning spoke wearily.

'Okay!' McCall shook himself into action. 'I'll turn out the town and have a search made. But whoever it is will be long gone now. You get some lights on in here, Chet, and see what you can find.'

'I'll have to visit the doc first,' Manning retorted.

'You took a slug?' There was sudden alarm in McCall's tones.

86

'Left arm. It can't be serious! You carry on and I'll look after myself.'

McCall departed, cursing, and Manning left the house by the front door, pausing on the sidewalk, staring at the men who were standing around, having heard the shots. He started along the street, and when he reached the hotel he saw Rosa standing in a group with several other women, and some of them were calling questions to the men who were passing.

When she saw Manning, Rosa became very still, and her face was pale in the light coming from the hotel windows. He went to her side and she clutched at him, drawing back when he winced.

'Are you all right?' she demanded. 'There were rumours that you and the marshal were involved in the shooting.'

'That's right.' He glanced down at his left arm and saw a dark stain of blood just below the shoulder on the outside of the arm. Pain was already lancing through the area, but he suspected that the wound was merely superficial.

'You've been hurt!' There was shock in her voice, but she immediately grasped his sleeve and ripped it up, exposing the bullet wound. Other women clustered around, peering at the arm, and Manning grinned slightly as he turned towards the hotel.

'It's not serious,' he said. 'A bandage will fix it up good.'

'I'll take care of it for you.' Rosa took his arm and they went into the hotel.

He sank down upon her bed when they reached her room and watched her intent face as she attended his wound. He satisfied himself that it was a flesh wound, and despite the fact that it was not serious it was beginning to give him hell. He gritted his teeth, fighting down the nameless fears that tried to flood into his mind.

'Thanks, Rosa,' he said, when she had completed her ministrations. He got to his feet and drew his gun, checking it, reloading the used chambers, and when he glanced up at her he saw she was staring at the big weapon with apprehension in her dark eyes. 'Does a gun scare you?' he asked.

'You've killed men with that, haven't you?' she countered.

'More than a few. But only because it was their lives or mine. That's how it is in these parts.'

She nodded slowly. 'I'm not accustomed to the wildness of

life out here. I expect it will take me some time to get used to it.'

'Does that mean you're planning on sticking around?' he demanded eagerly, and she smiled slowly as she nodded.

'I think I would be foolish to leave right now, with so much happening!'

He nodded, smiling, holstering the big .45 as he turned to the door.

'I'll see you later,' he said in a clipped tone. 'I have some unfinished business to handle.'

'If that bullet had been aimed six inches farther to the right it would have pierced your heart, Chet,' she said. 'Doesn't that thought worry you?'

'A great deal,' he replied, still smiling, but his lips were stiff, and he left her abruptly and went on down to the street.

There were a number of men engaged in a search of the town, and lanterns moved here and there through the shadows. Manning paused on the sidewalk and looked around, breathing heavily, his hand upon the butt of his holstered gun. He had no doubt that Grat Trimble was the man who shot him. Trimble had returned to his home for something or other, probably money, and it had been a close call. But Manning was no longer concerned about how close he had been to death. He was wondering if Glory Harpe had accompanied Trimble into town. The two seemed to have got together for some evil purpose, and he could only guess at that. They both wanted him dead!

But was the girl out there in the shadows, awaiting her chance to cut him down without warning? Manning shrugged, no longer indecisive and nervous. He drew a sharp breath as he felt his old determination pulsing through his mind, and a tight grin came to his hard lips. He ignored the pain in his left arm and it seemed to subside, as if the raw nerve ends were aware that he had recovered from the most recent test of his courage.

Going along to the law office, he found Barney McCall there, directing the search, and men were entering and leaving the office in a constant stream, forming part of a search pattern that was intended to cover the whole town.

'How you doing, Barney?' he demanded.

'I got the search going. What about you?'

'Nothing to brag about. A deep flesh wound.' There was a strong note in Manning's voice, and McCall shook his head in admiration.

'I'd like to know where the hell you get your nerve from,' he commented. 'You tried to kid me that you were nervous before you went into Trimble's house.'

Manning smiled but made no reply. He turned to the door, intent upon carrying out his own search of the town, but the door opened and Grat Trimble entered the office followed by a grinning townsman who was holding a levelled sixgun. Manning caught his breath as he looked into Trimble's haggard face, and did not miss the expression of hatred which flashed into the older man's dark eyes.

'Look what I got!' the townsman cried. 'Found a couple of saddle horses out of town in the area you told me to search, Marshal, and after I waited a few minutes Trimble showed up.'

'Good work, Billy!' McCall got to his feet and moved around the desk to face Trimble, who stared at Manning with a cold, unblinking gaze. 'I figured we'd see you again, Trimble,' he went on. 'Where's Glory Harpe?'

'Who's she?' Trimble countered.

McCall shook his head slowly as he searched Trimble, and when the sheaf of greenbacks appeared he tightened his lips.

'You didn't get these out of your house,' he said. 'I cleaned out your safe after you were arrested and put that money I found into your bank account. You've been to see Belling, huh? Did he give you this money or did you steal it?' He paused but Trimble did not reply. 'Billy, get over to Belling's house and check with him,' McCall ordered. 'See if he's okay and find out if Trimble was at his place tonight.'

The townsman nodded and departed hurriedly. McCall motioned for Trimble to sit down and the freighter did so, sighing heavily as he leaned back, his eyes still on Manning's alert face.

'You've got a lot to answer for already, Trimble,' McCall said. 'You've made a real mess of your life. After Glory Harpe busted you and Trig Forbes out of jail you went on a stealing spree!'

'I don't know anything about stealing!' Trimble retorted. 'How come you're trying to pin that on me?'

'We know a lot,' Manning cut in. 'For instance, Forbes and three other men hit the bank in Gadson Flats today, and Hart Loman was shot dead!'

'You're kidding!' Trimble's face paled as he stared first at

Manning, then at the watchful lawman.

'I wish it was a joke,' McCall said. 'You're mixed up in this bad business, Trimble. It's a pity, because you might have got out of jail in a couple of years if you'd stayed inside when Glory showed up to bust you out. What did she want you for? Why did you three team up?' His gaze flickered to Manning's face for a moment. 'I'll tell you why,' he continued remorselessly. 'You and Glory both hate Chet Manning. You both figured to drop on to him sometime when he wasn't expecting it, and you planned to kill him!'

'That's a lie!' Trimble shook his head slowly. 'I don't know a damn thing. Okay, so Glory busted me out of jail. I can't deny that! But we parted soon after. I've been laying low ever since! I sneaked back into town tonight in the hope of grabbing some of my dough and getting clear of the country. I'm all washed up around here and I figured to haul my freight. That's all I can tell you.'

A townsman came into the office, carrying a bundle of clothes, and he dropped them on the desk. There was a pair of saddlebags slung across his shoulder.

'Got these off the hosses that were with Trimble,' he said.

McCall looked over the clothes, then cast a quick glance at Manning. His eyes were bright as he returned his gaze to Trimble's defiant features.

'Who's the woman you're running around with, Trimble?' the marshal demanded. He paused and waited for a reply, but Trimble remained silent, his thin lips pinched, his dark eyes glittering. McCall sighed and opened the saddlebags, tipping out the contents on to the desk. He picked up a bible and opened it, studying the fly leaf. 'Glory Harpe,' he read loudly. 'I guess that proves you're lying, Trimble. Where is she now?'

'I don't know!'

'Okay.' McCall did not waste any time. 'You know where the cells are. On your way, Trimble! You'll have plenty of time to reflect upon your mistakes. Glory is around somewhere and we'll find her. She doesn't have a horse now, and we can search the town thoroughly come morning.'

Manning remained motionless while the marshal locked Trimble in a cell. When McCall returned to the office there was a grin on his heavy face.

'I figure this incident has taken some of the sting out of your problems, Chet,' he commented. 'I figure Glory is around here someplace, and we should be able to pick her up now. I've posted guards around the town to watch for trouble, and if she is sneaking around we'll get her. But what about Trig Forbes? You figure he cut off by himself after they busted him out of jail?'

'He certainly wasn't with them today!' Manning retorted. 'I wouldn't like to make a guess, Barney. But I'm not taking any chances. I'll wire my office and have a couple of my men sent out here. I want to get on the trail of Forbes as soon as I can. If he's teamed up with some more outlaws then we're gonna be right back where we were before Yaro's gang was smashed.'

McCall nodded. 'Meanwhile I want Glory Harpe, and I'll pull this town apart to get her.'

'I'll get along to the railroad depot and send my wires.' Manning smiled thinly, relieved by the developments. 'I'll be back in the morning to talk to Trimble after he's had the chance to think over the situation. If we can get some information from him then so much the better. But let me know if you pick up Glory, Barney.'

'Will do!'

Manning left the office and walked along the sidewalk to the depot. He kept a close watch upon his surroundings, feeling a sense of vulnerability as he considered Glory Harpe. The death of Ben Yaro had evidently disturbed her mind, and Manning was tight-lipped as he considered the past, when there had been a close relationship between him and the outlaw's wife. But she had been used cold-bloodedly to get him into a gun trap and there had never been any regard for him in her mind.

He sent his wire to Buffalo Junction, knowing there would be a reply by morning, and then he started back to the hotel. He needed to get a good night's sleep, for from tomorrow there would be plenty of activity. There was an eagerness inside him, and relief had settled in the back of his mind. His nerve had returned, and for that he was thankful.

As he passed an alley mouth close to the hotel a voice called to him, and Manning tensed as he paused, for it was a woman's voice. A shiver passed along his spine.

'Stand still, Manning, I've got my gun on you!' There was a vibrant note in the voice, and he recognised it as Glory's. He stood motionless, his hands at his sides.

'Glory, I've been hoping to come up with you,' he said. 'Let's go somewhere to talk.'

'There's nothing to be said between us,' she responded. 'You got what's coming to you aimed right at your back, and if it's the last thing I do I'll kill you.'

'Okay! I understand how you feel! But I reckon we could talk. You'd only be throwing your life away if you killed me, and you deserve better than that, Glory. I didn't know you were Ben Yaro's wife. And I'm the one who should be angry. You led me by the nose into a gun trap. Anyway, I didn't want to kill Yaro. I would have been happy to take him alive. I tried for a wing shot! But he was intent on putting me down and I didn't have time to nick him. Come on, Glory, let's go somewhere to talk. If you're set on killing me then you can do it later. But you ought to know that Trimble is back in town, and in jail. You rode in with him, huh? What are you after?'

'You! Me and Trimble want the same thing. You dead and in your grave!'

'Where does Trig Forbes fit into your plans?'

'Forbes?' Her voice was nervous, taut, and Manning could imagine her finger trembling on the trigger. Sweat broke out on his forehead. 'What about him?'

'We know you busted him and Trimble out of jail in Buffalo Junction, Glory! You're getting yourself into an almighty bad situation. Forbes hit the bank in Gadson Flats with three other men, and Hart Loman was shot dead!'

'No!'

'You think I would lie about that?' Manning spoke sharply, still motionless, but his mind was beginning to work normally once more and he was wondering how he could get off the end of the gun that threatened to blast him.

'When did this happen?' she demanded.

'Early this afternoon. You figure to gun me down in cold blood, huh? I can understand how you feel about me, Glory, and if you want to kill me then go ahead. I can't do anything about that. But don't get innocent people killed! You busted Forbes out of jail and he's killed Loman. Who else will he kill before he's put down?'

'That's got nothing to do with me,' she retorted. 'Step back into the cover of this alley mouth, and don't make the mistake of trying to outsmart me. I'm gonna kill you, but not here. I want to watch your face when I give it to you in the belly. I want you to die slow so I can enjoy your agony.'

'A man can only die!' he retorted, and there was a fine sheen of cold sweat beading his forehead.

'If you could die a hundred times over it wouldn't be enough for me!' she said vehemently. 'And the railroad will pay for what happened to Yaro. Me and Trimble were gonna make you all pay.'

'You won't be able to bust Trimble out of jail again,' Manning warned. 'Why don't you forget about this, Glory? You've got to give yourself time to get over the shock of Yaro's death. I know what you must be feeling. But those feelings will change later.'

'I'll never change!'

'You figure you're innocent?' he queried, moving backwards a pace at a time until he had gained the alley mouth. 'You were setting me up for Yaro, remember!'

'Who is that gal you were with at the hotel?'

'Rosa Mozee. She's Ike Mozee's daughter! He's the construction camp boss out at the end of track. He was wounded in that big attack. That's how guilty Yaro was. Over fifty men were killed that morning. I merely killed a snake when I nailed Yaro!'

'You made a big man of yourself by getting my husband! But a big reputation won't save you! Now stand still until I've got your gun.'

'You won't get away, Glory!' he warned, keeping his voice calm. 'Like I told you, Trimble is in jail and your horse is gone. Why don't you stop this before you go too far to be able to turn back?'

'I've gone too far already. I'm in this up to my neck, and I won't rest until I've seen you die.' She paused, and Manning heard her take a deep breath. 'Now stand still. This gun will go off if you so much as blink.'

He waited in silence, and felt her hand at his right hip. His gun was taken and then she jabbed his spine with the muzzle of her weapon.

'On your way!' she commanded. 'Down the alley to the back lots, and if you want to live as long as possible then don't try anything smart. I won't miss, and I'm itching to pull the trigger now!'

Manning obeyed her, aware that while he could keep her talking there was a chance that she would either change her mind about shooting him or he might get the opportunity to overpower her. He walked steadily into the shadows of the alley, his hands raised to shoulder height, and the girl remained at his back, a silent threat to his life. When they reached the back lots it was so dark he could hardly see a hand in front of his face, and he paused, to get the muzzle of the gun jabbing into his back as a warning.

'Which way?' he demanded, tensing, summoning up his courage and determination, and as Glory motioned with the gun he pivoted to the left, swinging quickly, his left arm dropping to bring his elbow against her gunhand.

She cried out at the suddenness of the attack, and the .38 blasted raucously, stabbing the shadows with a long red tongue of flame. But Manning's elbow had nudged the weapon off target, and he clenched his teeth as his ears were battered by the heavy report. He did not hesitate, sledging up his right fist in a vicious arc, and his knuckles connected with her jaw, knocking her unconscious. He wrenched the gun out of her hand as she began to fall, and was breathing heavily as she collapsed to the ground.

For a moment he stood over her, his mind in a turmoil and he trembled at the narrowness of his escape. Then he dragged his gun from the waistband of her pants, stuck her .38 into his waistband, and lifted her bodily from the ground. She was only beginning to stir by the time he reached the street and started across to the law office, and by the time she had recovered her senses they were in the office, confronting Barney McCall.

It seemed the end of his problems as far as they were concerned, Manning was thinking as he listened to McCall questioning her. Now there only remained Trig Forbes to recapture, and when his men arrived he would take great pleasure in hunting down the big outlaw. He felt greatly relieved. It seemed that most of his fears were proving to be groundless! And when Forbes was in custody once more he could go back to his duty of ensuring that the S & W kept pushing on towards Apache Pass.

Chapter Nine

Trig Forbes rode steadily towards the hideout where he had met up with Arrel, Santor and Dillon, and he felt a strong sense of satisfaction as he considered the way the robbery had gone and the fact that he had been able to down Hart Loman. His thick lips twisted into a dusty grin and he hoped he had killed the Gadson Flats town marshal; he chuckled heavily as he patted the bulging gunny sack tied to his saddlehorn. He squinted his eyes as he peered around. Grains of dust stung his large, craggy face. There was a heat haze shimmering along the nearest ridges, and the white glare of the sun was blinding. He hated this section of New Mexico, where summer was a nightmare of heat and drought. The wilderness about him was semi-desert, burning and desolate, an unchanging scene of rocks, cactus, thorn bushes and mesquite.

Forbes considered running out on his new partners with the money he had, but the thought of more to come from a series of well organised raids made him change his mind. If he waited a bit he would have enough money to enable him to leave New Mexico for greener pastures, and his eyes shone with a lustful glitter as he considered the fleshpots of northern towns where he was practically unknown.

Then he thought of Glory and the glitter in his eyes intensified. He had plans for that girl, and until they had been carried out he was not going anywhere. He drew a harsh breath, trying to moisten his lips with his tongue. She wanted to see Chet Manning dead, and Manning was now in Gadson Flats. He narrowed his eyes as he rode on. But he would have to kill Trimble to shut the man's snivelling mouth and get rid of him.

He was tempted to ride on to the main hideout, where he had arranged to see Glory and Trimble, but knew he would need the help of Arrel and the others, and he pulled his lips into a thin

95

line as he made plans. He pushed his horse steadily, saving a little of its strength for any emergency, and two hours later he was riding into the hideout.

Forbes spent thirty minutes blotting out his tracks, then went to the shack and made some coffee. He tipped out the contents of the gunny sack and sorted it, finally counting it, arriving at a total of seven thousand four hundred and fifty dollars. There was a grin on his face as he stuffed the money back into the sack then looked around for a hiding place. He left the shack, intending to hide the money elsewhere, but the sound of approaching hooves alerted him and he dragged his sixgun clear of its holster, covering the trio bearing down upon him.

When he saw it was Arrel and the others he lowered the gun, watching them with a tight grin upon his face. They reined up in front of him, grinning, all elated by the success of their plan.

'I was just going to hide this until you showed up,' Forbes said, lifting the sack a little. He holstered his gun. 'Did you blot your tracks when you rode in?'

'Yep! An Injun couldn't track us in here,' Arrel retorted, stepping down from his saddle. He untied a sack from his saddlehorn. 'Let's put all the dough together and see what we come up with, huh?' He looked sideways at the stocky figure of Ben Santor. 'You got a good sackful, didn't you, Ben?'

'Sure did!' Santor grinned as he lifted a bulging bag from his saddle. 'I grabbed the real big notes. There are twenties and hundreds in here.'

Forbes's eyes glinted as they entered the shack.

'We did all right,' he commented. 'I reckon it's a good sign for us, boys. We've started as we mean to go on. After this we can hit the railroad.'

'You figure there ain't enough dough in the towns for us?' Arrel demanded, tipping the contents of his sack upon the table. 'The railroad is a different proposition, Trig! If we can do without it then so much the better. I spotted Chet Manning in town, and he ain't the kind of cuss I want to tangle with.'

'I got me a woman who's keen to see Manning dead!' Forbes retorted. 'I figured we could take care of that chore. With Manning gone we can do as we please around the railroad.'

'We'll see!' Arrel spoke without enthusiasm, and they fell to counting the money.

Snap Dillon used a pencil and a piece of paper to work out

the grand total, and came up with the staggering figure of thirty thousand dollars. There was silence as they looked at one another, then Forbes let out a whoop and grabbed up a double handful of money. His dark eyes glittered as he stared at his partners.

'This is only the start,' he said. 'There's plenty more around, and it's ours for the taking. But grab yourselves some food, boys, because I want to ride on to the main hideout. We'll be safer there, and we can take our time making plans.'

They ate, chatting gleefully, filled with high spirits, already making plans for spending some of the money, and Forbes let his thoughts drift along the well worn trail in his mind which usually led to women.

It was dark when they rode out, and the money had been split into quarter shares and handed out. Forbes led the way, following his instincts, squinting at the features he had marked in his mind to enable him to find his way around the barren wilderness. They rode for six hours, and dawn was greying the sky when they halted for breakfast. When the sun came up they went on, pushing steadily for their distant goal, and two more days passed before they came eventually to the main hideout.

Forbes rode on ahead to check out the gully and the hideout, and although he was pleased to find no signs of strangers around, his heavy features stiffened when he spotted the outgoing tracks that marked Glory and Trimble's departure days before. Fearing the worst, he pushed on into the canyon and came upon the shack where they should be. The place was deserted, and he sat staring around, a terrible rage rising up inside him as he considered having lost Glory. For some moments he remained stock-still, clenching his big hands, his eyes bulging with fury. Then he dismounted and kicked open the door of the shack, striding in and pausing on the threshold. He looked for a note, or any indication of their intentions. He found nothing and departed quickly, returning to where the others were waiting impatiently for him.

'What's wrong?' Arrel demanded, glimpsing Forbes's expression.

'They're gone! Glory and that skunk Trimble. The danged fools! They'll run into trouble if they're not careful.'

'Is it safe for us to stay here?' Santor demanded, glancing around. 'If they get picked up will they talk about this place?'

'Hell no!' Forbes shook his head. 'I reckon Trimble talked the girl into going to Jules Crossing with him. He's got a freightline office there. Maybe they've gone to pick up some dough, huh? Trimble was bellyaching about having nothing. You fellers can ride in now and make yourselves at home. I'm going on to Jules Crossing.'

'That woman must mean something to you, Trig,' Arrel observed.

'That's right. I want her back!' Forbes's dark eyes filled with a ferocious glitter. 'I'll kill that fool Trimble if anything happens to her.'

'How long you figure to be gone?' Snap Dillon asked.

'Four days to Jules Crossing from here,' Forbes mused. 'I'll stay mebbe one night, then four days back.'

'Hell, we ain't gonna sit around some crummy hideout for nine days waiting for you to show!' Santor rasped.

'You wanta go along with me?' Forbes demanded.

'Anything would be better than sitting around here playing cards and losing my share of the loot to Arrel and Dillon,' Santor retorted. 'Anyways, you can't ride into Jules Crossing, Trig. You're too well knowed in this neck of the woods, ain't you?'

'That's about the weight of it,' Forbes admitted.

'Then let's rest up the nags tonight and ride out tomorrow,' Arrel suggested. 'We can all do with a break, and this dough is sure burning a hole in my pockets. We ain't so well known around here, Trig, and we can go into any town and get away with it, if we're careful.'

'Yeah?' Forbes sighed heavily. 'Well mebbe it's a good thing we teamed up after all. I'll go along with what you say, boys! We'll rest up tonight and ride out in the morning.'

They headed into the hideout and camped, and at dawn, after breakfast, they took to the trail again, riding out in a different direction, making for the distant town of Jules Crossing. It took them four days to reach it, and on the evening of the fourth day they reined up on a ridge overlooking the town and sat their mounts, stubbled and dusty, hung over their saddles from the exertions of the hard ride.

'Hell, I'm gonna get me a barrel of beer, hop into a tub with it, and lay soaking all night, inside and out,' Santor said. 'Then

98

tomorrow I'm gonna buy me a whole new outfit from the store and enjoy myself for a week or two.'

'We're not stopping over,' Forbes retorted. 'I ain't camping outside of town while you fellers soak up all the pleasures. I can't show my face inside of town limits without having that tough marshal Barney McCall either shooting me or throwing me in jail.'

'You ain't scared of no town marshal, are you, Trig?' Santor demanded.

'You know better than that,' Forbes retorted. 'I killed a town marshal a few days ago, remember. But too many of them fellers falling down in the dust is likely to start a lot of trouble around here. I got a couple of places I can sneak into around town, but I ain't able to ride in openly, so you fellers will have to look around and find out for me if Trimble and Glory showed up. I figure this is the first place they would make for. They was both dead keen on killing Chet Manning, and he's always around some town or other in this area.'

'Okay, Trig,' Arrel said. 'We'll find out about them. Now where do we see you again?'

There's a cantina in the poor part of town belonging to a Mex called Martinez,' Forbes said. 'One of you can find me there. Ask for Mama Maria and she'll bring you to me.'

'Okay.' Santor was impatient to get to town. He set spurs into his mount and rode down the rocky slope. 'Come on, *amigos*, let's go get our share of drinking and gambling and whatever else they got to offer saddle tramps.'

Forbes sat his mount and watched their departure, and his brown eyes were slitted, his mind working. He was already thinking of Mama Maria, and a tremor started through him as his passions began to rise. He would save Glory until later, much later, and in the meantime he had enough dough to have himself a whale of a time. He waited until darkness had fallen before skirting the town and riding in across the back lots to the Martinez Cantina.

There was a dilapidated barn behind the cantina, and Forbes took his horse inside, putting it away and taking care of it although he burned with impatience as his imagination conjured up pictures of what awaited him inside the cantina. He carried his money in the sack as he finally headed for the back door, and paused only long enough to peer through a window into the grimy kitchen.

There was a big halfbreed woman cooking at the stove, and Forbes's eyes glittered as he took in her ample lines. When she turned from the stove and moved to the table he licked his lips at the sight of her heavy bosom, and the thin, lowcut dress she was wearing did not conceal much of her upper body. He thrust open the door and entered the kitchen swiftly, surprising the woman, dropping his sack and grabbing her with all his strength. She squealed, turning to strike at him, but when she recognised him her face lost its fear and took on an expression of shocked surprise.

'*Madre Dios!*' she gasped. 'Senor Trig! But I heard you were killed with the rest of the gang.'

'Not me, Mama Maria,' he said with a grin. 'I'm still alive and kicking, and here in the flesh.' He squeezed her, embracing her heavy figure with lustful vigour. 'I'll be staying for a few days, so fetch Martinez so I can talk to him, and gimme a bottle of your best tequila. I got a sack full of dough and some time to spend it.'

He slapped her large rump and she laughed in a high-pitched voice, hurrying from the kitchen, gazing back at him with dark, greedy eyes. Forbes took a deep breath as he stared around the kitchen. This was the nearest place to home that he knew, and he was happy here.

Martinez came hurrying into the kitchen, a tall, swarthy Mexican of around forty, with dark features showing a great deal of concern.

'Senor Forbes!' he exclaimed. 'I am very glad to see you alive. We all thought you were killed. That Senor Manning made a big clean-up on your gang.'

'But he didn't get me, Martinez!' Forbes said in his booming voice, and he slapped the Mexican's shoulder. 'I figure on sticking around for a couple of days, and I want all the usual services. Mama Maria forgets her cooking until I go. I'll be needing her.'

'But, senor, things have changed around here since your last visit.' Martinez clasped his hands together as if about to pray. 'The railroad troubleshooters are in town, and everyone is on the watch for trouble. Mama Maria is now promised to Miguel del Soro, and he is a very jealous man. He is across the border

100

at the moment, but is due to return at any time.'

'That cattle thief?' There was disgust in Forbes's voice. 'I'll take up with him when he gets back. I don't want any trouble around here, Martinez!' He snatched up his sack and produced a handful of notes, thrusting them into the Mexican's greedy hands without bothering to count them. 'There you are! Take care of my needs. Keep me supplied, Martinez, and keep the change when I leave. We're good friends. I take care of you and you take care of me. Now I need a bath and your best room. Come on, Mama Maria, you can scrub my back.'

Martinez sighed heavily as he thrust the money into his pockets. He met Forbes's dark gaze, and nodded reluctantly.

'We are very good friends, Senor Trig!' he said. 'I take good care of your interests. But if Miguel del Soro comes back before you leave then you will have to fight him. I would prefer no trouble in my cantina, you understand. The law is strict in this town. Marshal McCall is one *mal hombre!*'

'If he gives you any trouble then let me know!' Forbes rasped, putting an arm around Mama Maria's big shoulders. He waved the gunny sack under the Mexican's nose. 'I got plenty more dough, and I ain't gonna stop spending until it's all gone. I figure I got some more for you if you watch out for me! No double-crossing, Martinez! I reckon you understand me, huh?'

'I understand you well, Senor Trig!' Martinez replied.

'Good. Then there won't be any trouble!' Forbes almost lifted Mama Maria from her feet as he swung towards the door. But he paused as a thought crossed his mind, and some of his good humour fled as he stared at the Mexican. 'Say, you know just about everything that goes on around Jules Crossing, Martinez,' he said. 'I lost a couple of friends of mine a few days ago. Have you heard if they've shown up around here?'

'Friends of yours, Senor Trig? What are their names?'

'Grat Trimble and Glory Harpe!'

'But of course,' Martinez nodded. 'You lost your friends because they are both in the calaboose! Chet Manning was in town.'

'How's that?' Forbes was so shocked he let his arm fall from Maria's heavy shoulders.

Martinez explained how Trimble and Glory had been arrested, and Forbes cursed and slammed a big fist against the flimsy wall, shaking adobe loose from the low ceiling.

'Damn that Chet Manning!' he snarled in a husky tone. 'I guess something will have to be done about him. Glory was right! There won't be no peace around here until he's dead! Is Manning still in town?'

'No, senor. He brought in some of his men, left one here, and went out to search for you.'

'Search for me?' Forbes scowled. 'Where did he ride?'

'They plan to look in all the old hideouts Yaro used.'

'Figuring that I'd still be using them, huh?' A tight grin pulled at Forbes's thick lips. 'That's okay, Martinez. You send someone along to the saloons. I got three *gringo* friends in town – Arrel, Santor and Dillon. Get word to them that I want to see them here, but not for a couple of hours. I got some important things to do before I bust Glory and Trimble out of jail. I guess they'll keep for a spell, huh?'

'I'll see that your friends learn of your desire to see them, Senor Trig!' Martinez nodded emphatically.

'But not before midnight, huh?' Forbes chuckled, and thrust Mama Maria through the doorway ahead of him.

They went up to her room and Forbes closed the door. He removed his gunbelt and unbuckled his pants. Lying on the bed, he motioned for Mama Maria to finish undressing him, and she did so eagerly. When he was stripped he motioned for her to do the same, and watched avidly as her large figure was revealed. Her flesh was darkly tanned, and she had large breasts and voluptuous hips. Forbes moistened his lips, feeling his pulses begin to race as he beckoned her to the side of the bed.

He caught her by the wrist and pulled her on to the bed, pushing her flat and parting her thighs, working his hand between her fleshy limbs. Then he lay back and pulled her across him, forcing her legs open and on either side of his own, making her sit astride and do the work. He grunted as she brought him to erection, and she crouched over him, intent upon giving him pleasure, gyrating her sensuous hips to and fro, causing him to grasp the sides of the bed and jerk convulsively. He lost control and was lost in an exploding orgasm which drained him of his ardour. Sweat ran down his face as he relaxed and pulled her to one side, holding her tightly while he awaited a resumption of his desire.

He swigged from the bottle at his side and thought of the things he would do to Glory when he saw her again. He drowsed pleasantly until Mama Maria warned him the time was around midnight. He yawned and stretched, for he was tired, but he rolled off the bed and stood up.

'Go down and see if my *amigo* has arrived,' he commanded. 'If he has then give him a drink and tell him I won't be long. When I've settled some business I got to attend to I'll come back here and finish you off, okay?'

The woman nodded and departed as he pulled on his clothes. Minutes later Forbes descended the stairs and went into Martinez's private apartment. Hemp Arrel got to his feet. The outlaw had cleaned himself up. He had been drinking but was not drunk or even unsteady. His pale eyes glittered as they studied Forbes's heavy countenance.

'I got your message, Trig,' he said. 'What's on your mind?'

'Did you learn anything about Glory and Trimble?'

'Sure. They're both in jail. I figured that they'll keep for a couple more days. Me and the boys are doing some celebrating in a quiet way.'

'Well I figure we don't have any time to waste,' Forbes retorted. 'We got to get ourselves set up around here, and I reckon we can do that now.' He went on to explain that Chet Manning was out searching the hideouts. 'I reckon we can bust that jail now and get those two out of it. Then we'll light out. We got work to do, Hemp. The time for celebrating will come later.'

'I'll go along with that,' Arrel retorted. 'But I figure Dillon and Santor won't be eager to pull out before morning.'

'You know where they are?'

'Sure! They both took on a skinful of liquor and then retired to a place down this end of Mainstreet called Cantina Dolores. I don't reckon they'll be fit for anything until the sun comes up, Trig!'

'Yeah?' Forbes looked impatient for a moment, then shook his head. 'I guess they need to let off steam, huh? And I better look around before going into this like a bull.' He grinned. 'Okay, Hemp. Come and see me in the morning, not too early. I'm going out now to take a look around.'

'Be careful,' Arrel warned. 'I heard a lot of talk in the

saloon about you. The sheriff has sent a deputy to Gadson Flats, and they're raising dust looking for you.'

'Good. While they're out looking we can stick around here. I don't figure they'll think we're in town.' Forbes smiled happily. 'We got to stay quiet, Hemp, so warn your boys not to make any trouble. I'll see you in the morning.'

'I'll be here around nine.' Arrel departed immediately.

Forbes considered for a moment and, when Mama Maria returned from showing Arrel out, he prepared to leave.

'Where you going at this time of night?' she demanded. 'You no like Mama Maria? You go look for other girl?'

'You know me better than that!' he retorted, grinning, slapping her hard across the rump. 'I'll be back pronto, but I got some work to do that won't wait until morning. Watch for me, Mama Maria, and if that greaser Miguel shows up tell him I'll carve my initials on his windpipe.' He clenched his big hands for a moment, his eyes glinting, then relaxed and departed.

Jules Crossing was dark, although lanterns threw yellow pools of light at irregular intervals along the main street. Forbes kept to the shadows, moving stealthily towards the jail, and he watched for signs of the lawman he knew would be making a round of the town. There was a light in the law office, and he stood opposite, staring at it for long moments while his mind turned over the facts. Glory was in jail and he meant to bust her out – not because she had busted him out once and he wanted to repay the favour: it was the woman herself that was the attraction.

It must have been Trimble's fault that they fell into the hands of the law again, Forbes told himself, and his lips pulled tight as he imagined having Trimble's scrawny neck in his grip. He exhaled sharply as tension built up in his mind, and when the law office door suddenly opened and Barney McCall appeared, pausing to lock the door behind him, Forbes grinned. He watched the town marshal set off along the street towards the saloons, and when the street was quiet again, Forbes crossed it, losing himself in the shadows around the jail.

Peering through a window in the alley, he discovered that the front office was empty. So McCall didn't have a deputy or a night jailer! He made a note of the fact and moved along the alley to the rear of the jail. There was a barred window in the back wall and he peered through it, finding himself looking into the cells. A lantern was alight in the corridor, throwing a feeble yellow light into the cells. Forbes spotted figures on the bunks in a couple of the cells, and his eyes glistened as he made out Glory's features. The woman was lying on her side, her face towards the window, and she was in a deep sleep. She had thrust off her blanket because of the hot night, and Forbes let his gaze devour her slender lines. He moistened his lips. He needed that female!

The window was overlooking her cell, and Forbes tensed as he pressed his face close to the bars. McCall wouldn't be back for some time. He could talk to Glory, let her know that help was on hand, and his breathing quickened as he hissed hoarsely in an attempt to awaken her. But he dared not make too much noise, and after several moments gave up the attempt. For some time he stood in the darkness, considering the situation, and then decided that he could wait no longer. He had to bust Glory out of jail now, and the easiest way of doing that was by ambushing the town marshal, taking his keys and just unlocking the place.

He grinned, eager for action, and turned immediately, ready to carry out his plan. But as he moved a harsh voice called softly to him from the surrounding shadows, and the ominous click of a sixgun being cocked came to his ears. He froze as a figure materialised, and light from the window flickered upon a levelled gun. He did not need to be told to raise his hands, for he did so instinctively, with fatalistic calm . . .

Chapter Ten

During the days that followed the capture of Trimble and Glory Harpe, Manning found life rigorous. He questioned both prisoners several times and failed to gain admissions from either, and when Joe Carver and Hank Bolden arrived in Jules Crossing in response to his wire, Manning began to make plans for searching the area for Forbes.

But Manning found himself with an instinctive dislike of Hank Bolden. There was something about the big man that he could not accept, and when he looked into Bolden's brooding face and saw the pinched expression on the thin lips, he felt a pang of concern. He had always trusted his instincts and they had never led him far wrong. But Bolden was an ex-detective! Manning shook his head as he confronted both men at the station when they stepped off the train. Why had Bolden quit the detective agency in Texas?

'Glad to see you, Chet!' Joe Carver greeted him, grinning his usual wide smile. 'You took another slug, I heard. Hope it ain't serious.'

'Nothing that will stop me, Joe,' Manning replied. 'Will you go along the street and have a talk with Barney McCall? You do know Barney, don't you?'

'Sure! Me and Barney are old friends. He was town marshal at Sourdough Creek before he came here, and I got to know him well. What do you want me to do?'

'There are a couple of prisoners in the jail; Glory Harpe, Yaro's widow, and Grat Trimble. Perhaps a new approach might get something out of them. I figure they were hooked up with Trig Forbes but I can't get it out of them. Work on them, Joe, and I'll check with you shortly.'

'Okay!' The tall troubleshooter departed instantly, leaving Manning gazing at the harshly set features of Hank Bolden.

'Well!' Bolden declared. 'I'm a stranger around here so I can't be useful in the way that Carver is. But you mentioned Trig Forbes. I knew a Trig Forbes five or six years back in Texas. He was a crook dealing in any crime he could handle. I don't suppose there could be two badmen with a name like Trig Forbes, so it's likely this *hombre* is the man I know, huh?'

Manning described Forbes and Bolden nodded slowly.

'Yeah, that sounds like my man. He got away from me once. I'd sure like to meet up with him again.'

'I heard tell that prisoners don't hardly ever get away from you, Bolden!' Manning said quietly, and saw the big man's lips pull tight. The insolent expression became more pronounced as Bolden grinned.

'Who's been talking about me?' he demanded.

'You scared about what people might have to say about you?'

'Nope! I got nothing to hide. I was a detective along the border for a couple of years, and I got thrown in with a lot of tough people. Stories do get around, but you must know that a lot of them can't be true. I expect there are a lot of tales about you!'

'That's right.' Manning still felt uneasy about the man. 'Why did you leave Butterfield?'

'I told you when I saw you at Big Bend. They cramped my style.'

'That's not good enough for me!' Manning sharpened his tone. 'I can find out easy enough, but I'd prefer to hear it from you. So you're a man who prefers to bring in his prisoners dead! A lot of men are like that! I won't hold that against you when the dead men are of Trig Forbes's ilk. But when you shoot up old railroad employees who do nothing more than lift a little freight in a weak moment then I have to regard you as a risk to our operations, a liability that we can't afford.'

'I heard you run a tough outfit!'

'That's right. On the last big operation against Ben Yaro I lost all three of my assistant troubleshooters!'

'Maybe they should have shot first and asked questions afterwards!' Bolden suggested, his grin widening. 'It might be they'd still be alive today. But I'll tell you this much, Manning. You can depend on me in any tight spot. If you have to go in shooting and I'm there then you'll have to be fast to stay ahead of me. I know my way around! I don't think you can afford to

107

hunt down Trig Forbes without me. I know a lot about that particular badman.'

'Okay, I've got an open mind,' Manning said. 'I'm listening. What can you tell me about Forbes?'

'He's part crazy!' Bolden nodded when he saw Manning's frown. 'Yeah! He's not just an out-and-out robber. He'll gun a man down just for the hell of it when he's got blood in his eyes, and if he gets his hands on a woman there's not much left of her when he's done.'

'The law will be out after him,' Manning said. 'But we want him for the train robbery and murdering company employees.'

'Tell me what you want me to do.'

'We're riding out of here,' Manning said. 'I want to get after Forbes and the three bank robbers with him as soon as we can. There's a train back to Gadson Flats at midday and we'll be on it. We'll try and pick up Forbes's trail. In the meantime you can take a walk around this town and make yourself familiar with its layout.'

'Okay, I'll be back here before noon.' Bolden grinned and departed, walking towards the street, leaving Manning staring after him with a thoughtful expression on his face. The big man swung his massive shoulders and exuded an atmosphere of insolence and menace.

Manning did not move until Bolden had disappeared from his sight. Then he went to the street and made his way to the law office. He found Joe Carver and McCall inside, chatting together, and for a moment Manning forgot his feelings about Bolden.

'I've been getting filled in on what's been happening around here, Chet,' Carver said, straightening his tall frame, the habitual grin on his lean face. 'You want me to have a talk with the prisoners now?'

'Yeah, you do that, Joe. We're leaving for Gadson Flats on the train at noon, so be ready to catch it. We're taking out after Forbes and those others. But I'm concerned about the link between Glory, Trimble and Forbes. I got a nasty feeling that if Forbes learns we've got these two in jail he might come in here to return the favour Glory did him.'

'Just let them try!' McCall said in heavy, eager tones.

'Sure,' Manning nodded. 'But if they drop on to you, Barney, you won't know much about it.' He glanced at Carver, who was watching him intently. 'Joe, have you changed your mind any about Hank Bolden since I talked to you last?'

'Not an inch,' came the soft reply. 'I don't like that man and I ain't making a secret of the fact. You've got to watch him, Chet.'

'Yeah. I got the same kind of feeling about him.' Manning spoke slowly. 'There's something about Bolden I just don't cotton to. When I get back to Buffalo Junction I'm gonna find out why he turned in his detective badge. He's a killer! But we can't hold that against him! However I ain't taking him along with us when we ride out. I figure to leave Bolden around here in case Forbes and his new gang show up to try and bust our prisoners out. Barney, you keep an eye on Bolden, huh?'

'Sure, if you say!' The town marshal nodded. 'Do you have anything at all against him?'

'Nothing, and that's what makes it tough on me!' Manning grimaced. 'I've got to give him his chance, but my instincts are against him. Just watch him, Barney, and don't let him know it.'

'Uhuh!' McCall nodded. 'So you're both pulling out of here on the noon train! What about Rosa Mozee? Is she sticking around?'

'I'm on my way to talk to her while Joe is talking to the prisoners,' Manning said. 'I expect Rosa will go back to Buffalo Junction now.'

'She's a mighty fine gal,' McCall observed, his dark eyes glinting. 'Some lucky guy will get her for a wife.' He grinned at Manning. 'You look like you're powerful friendly with her. I reckon you could do a lot worse for yourself, Chet.'

Manning smiled as he shook his head, and for a moment he felt awkward. Then his grin widened.

'I guess we all know that wives and troubleshooting don't go together,' he said, turning to the street. 'Have a chat with those two in the cells, Joe, and we'll compare notes later. Be ready to board the train at noon!'

Carver nodded and followed McCall into the cells. Manning left the office and went to the hotel, finding Rosa in her room. She was looking prettier than ever, he noticed, and a pang went through him.

'Rosa, I have to leave town today. Two of my men have

arrived and I'm going back to Gadson Flats to pick up a horse. I'm riding out into the country for a week or so, and I reckon you'll want to go back to Buffalo Junction now, huh?'

'Yes.' She nodded, and he noticed that her features hardened a little at his news. 'I'm sorry you're going away. I hope it won't be dangerous for you!'

'I've got to come up with these badmen,' he said. 'The law will be out after them, but the county sheriff doesn't push himself at all and leaves most of the work to his chief deputy, who's young and inexperienced. If I don't go after Forbes then he may come looking for me, and that will cut down my chances. I prefer to fight his kind on my own terms.'

'I can understand that.' She nodded, her lips compressed. 'May I travel with you as far as Gadson Flats?'

'I shall look forward to your company,' he responded, smiling gently. 'Then I'll put you on the train to Buffalo Junction and tell the conductor to keep an eye on you.'

'I shan't forget the way you kept an eye on me when I first arrived,' she smiled. 'I was afraid of you, Chet, before I discovered who you were. I thought you could be a badman. You looked so big and tough, and the way you wore your gun seemed to suggest that you wouldn't hesitate to use it. Then the gambler! I was horrified when you had to step in. You threw him off the train while it was still in motion, didn't you?'

'That's right. It's a tough world out here, Rosa, and you better bear that in mind all the time. That gambler! After I threw him off the train, someone shot and robbed him!'

Her face showed shock, and Manning nodded grimly.

'That's the way it goes,' he said.

'Since I came here and met you and the other people my father knows and found out what life is like in these parts, I've got a different idea about the job you all do.' There was a muffled note in her voice that made it soft, as if emotion had constricted her throat. 'I shuddered when I thought of you going out day after day with a gun, ready to shoot down all the badmen who got in your way. But it isn't like that, is it, Chet?'

'No!' He shook his head slowly. 'We have to hunt down the men who threaten the railroad, and protect innocent people using it. In most cases, where the badmen are train robbers and killers, it's a fact that they are less than human. They won't let anyone stand in their way. They'll shoot down everyone

110

who doesn't obey them in a flash. They have to be hunted down like the animals they are!' Manning's voice deepened and his eyes glittered. 'If you stick around much longer, Rosa, you'll learn a great deal more about this country, and realise that much of it isn't pleasant.'

'I will pray for you,' she said softly. 'I won't be able to sleep nights for thinking about you while you're out there in the wilderness after those men.'

'Don't do it!' His harsh tone startled her. 'It isn't wise to become involved with a man like me.' He shook his head. 'I could get killed any time, and then you'd have nothing but misery. You just hold yourself apart from my kind, Rosa, and it won't hurt at all!'

'I don't think that's the right attitude,' she replied. 'I can understand it, but I don't think it is right. And I now believe my mother was wrong to leave my father because of his job. I can see this because I missed my father even though I never knew him well. I missed him all my life because he was not around. Now I've come to him I won't leave, and your way of life will become mine!'

'That's a brave attitude,' he said unsteadily, and fought down his emotions. He looked at her keenly, saw the message in her face, and knew she meant more to him than any girl he had ever known. He could not put a finger on it, but there was something about her that got under his skin and made him squirm. Netta had never affected him like this, although he had a lot of feeling for her. But their association was on a purely physical level and he knew it. But he dared not let Rosa know how he felt about her, and would not permit his personal feelings to overstep the strict control his grim training had placed upon them.

'It's a very lonely life if you try to cut yourself off from all human contact just because you might suffer if someone died,' she said wisely. 'Just think of the life my mother led because she left my father! She was afraid he might be killed, but she lived most of her life without him, as if he had died! I think that was a foolish thing to do. She ought to have made the most of the time they were both alive!'

Manning could think of no answer to that, but standing before her and looking into her serious face made him aware that she was a girl in a million, and he stifled his regrets and steeled himself against the impulse that was in him. He was lonely. He needed a wife! He wanted someone he could call his own, someone to turn to when the going got rough. But he would not admit that a man in his job could expect a woman to share the dangers and uncertainties of his life. While he remained on his own he did not have to answer to anyone for his actions, need not hesitate to make a life or death move for fear that he might die and cause pain to a loved one!

He closed his mind to the teeming thoughts and turned away. 'I've still got some things to take care of around here before I can pull out,' he said. 'But I'll come for you in time to catch the train, Rosa.'

'I'll be ready,' she promised.

Manning was thoughtful as he went out to the street, and he stood for some moments on the edge of the sidewalk, staring around at the ugly town shimmering in the heat of the morning. He saw Hank Bolden emerging from a store, and narrowed his blue eyes as he took in the big man's figure. Again he tried to decide what it was about Bolden that he did not like, and could not analyse his feelings. It was just a hunch that gripped him, and he stifled a sigh as he went after the man. He had to give Bolden the benefit of the doubt. Until he saw the man in action he could not pass judgement.

'Bolden!' Manning's voice was crisp as he called after the man when he drew closer, and was surprised by the way Bolden came spinning around, pulling his gun almost clear of its holster before the ex-detective recognised him.

Bolden shook his head and thrust the weapon deep into its holster. He grinned tightly as Manning paused in front of him.

'Must be getting old!' he commented sardonically. 'There's no reason why I should be so jumpy this far from the border!'

'You made a lot of enemies in your career as a detective, huh?' Manning demanded.

'I reckon so. No doubt you got a few around!'

'Two of them are in jail here. I wanted to tell you that I figure it would be better if you hung around here for a few days, just in case Forbes decides to show up. There might be three hardcases with him, and if they get word that Glory Harpe and Trimble are in jail they might come to bust them loose. I want you to keep your eyes open and back up the town

112

marshal should something break. Come along and meet Barney McCall.'

They went back along the sidewalk to the law office. Manning watched Bolden as he introduced the man to McCall, and again Bolden's smoothness seemed deceptive, his pale eyes at variance with the smiling expression on his face. But if Bolden did his job properly Manning would have no complaints.

Joe Carver came out of the cells, and shook his head when Manning looked inquiringly at him.

'Nothing doing,' the lean troubleshooter said in disgust. 'I don't think you're gonna get anything out of that pair, except that neither of them have got any love for you. If they ever get out of jail, Chet, don't let them get behind you.'

'Maybe I should have a talk with them,' Bolden suggested. 'I got a lot of experience in handling suspects.'

'I've heard of it,' Manning could not help saying, and saw the big man's eyes narrow slightly. 'But go ahead. You're staying on in Jules Crossing when we pull out. Wire Gadson Flats if anything comes up around here, and I'll arrange for the law there to pass on any messages.'

'Okay,' Bolden nodded. 'You can leave this end of it to me. I've had a lot of experience.'

'I'll be in touch with you later,' Manning said. He grinned at McCall and motioned for Joe Carver to come with him.

When they stood on the street, Carver looked into Manning's eyes and grimaced.

'The more I see of Bolden the less I like his manner,' he commented. 'When I look at him I get the idea I'm looking at a snake that's grinning and trying to be friendly while preparing to bite.'

'That's how I feel about him, but perhaps your warning about him before I even set eyes on him has coloured my mind against him.' Manning frowned. 'He's staying here so he can't get into much trouble. Let's go along to the depot.'

'It's a hell of a country out there,' Carver observed as they walked along the street.

'I know!' Manning grinned wryly. 'I've been over it a lot of times. But mebbe we'd better check out a couple of the hide-outs that I know about before we go any further. Go along to the stable, Joe, and rent two horses for a week. I think we'd better set out from here.'

'And Miss Mozee?' Carver demanded.

Manning pulled his lips into a thin line, undecided, but duty came first, as always, and he sighed heavily.

'We'll see her on the train before we leave, and the conductor will keep an eye on her. Get some supplies for us, Joe, and all the gear we might need. It's going to be tough.'

Carver nodded and departed, and Manning went on to the depot to send a wire to Asa Blaine. His mind was made up and he wanted to get into action. The rest of the morning passed all too quickly, and two saddled mounts were waiting in front of the law office as he walked Rosa along to the depot. There was a strange, unsettled feeling inside him as he waited with the girl for the train to arrive. It was coming from Gadson Flats, and would return there immediately. The conductor agreed to let Rosa have a seat in the baggage car and the moment for parting arrived.

Manning felt awkward, but smiled easily, and Rosa held out a slim hand to him, looking up into his face.

'I shall be worrying about you until you return to Buffalo Junction, Chet,' she told him softly. 'Will you wire Mr Blaine when you can to let him know how you're making out?'

'I'm afraid that won't be possible.' He shook his head ruefully. 'There are no telegraph offices where I'm going, but I'll take care of myself, don't you fear. I'll look forward to seeing you again when I return.'

Her hand lay in his for long moments, and he trembled at their contact. Then he helped her into the baggage car and she sat down and made herself comfortable. Manning felt a strange reluctance filling him as he left her, and when the train had gone he stood staring after it. A shadow fell across him and he looked around swiftly to see Hank Bolden standing nearby. There was a tight grin on the man's heavy face.

'She's a right pretty gal, Manning!' the ex-detective remarked. 'You'll need to keep a close eye on her with a badman like Trig Forbes around.'

'Forbes won't be around long enough to make himself a nuisance,' Manning retorted. 'I'm riding out with Carver now. Check with the telegraph office every so often for wires, and keep your eyes open around here.'

'I know my job!' Bolden said pointedly, and Manning suppressed a sigh and departed. Hearing an amused snicker from Bolden, he glanced back over his shoulder, but the big man was already turning away, and Manning compressed his lips, filled with sudden determination.

When he returned to Buffalo Junction he would make some enquiries about Hank Bolden, he promised himself, but right now there was a long, hot ride ahead of him and he needed all his wits and concentration upon what he had to do.

He rode out with Joe Carver, making for the hideouts he knew, and he figured it would be a long shot if Forbes happened to be in any of them. But long shots sometimes paid off, and it was his job to check out every eventuality. They rode west, making for the badlands, and the afternoon sun was a heavy burden upon them, baking them and sweating their vitality out through their pores. He could not help thinking of Rosa as they rode, and for the first time since he had taken up trouble-shooting his heart was not really in his work.

Chapter Eleven

Trig Forbes narrowed his eyes as the man with the levelled gun came silently towards him. His hands were at shoulder height, but his thick fingers curled, as if he had trouble resisting the impulse to make a play for his guns. The light coming from the barred window showed him a big man, someone almost as big as himself, and he knew it was not the town marshal, Barney McCall.

'Who in the hell are you, mister?' he demanded, and eased his hands downwards a fraction.

'You know me, Trig!' came the surprising reply, and a chuckle sounded. 'If you lower your hands another inch I'll put a bullet through your belt buckle. I want to talk to you, and you got nothing to worry about. I'm not a lawman.'

'Who are you?' Forbes repeated. Some of his cold shock had faded at the man's words. 'Why are you sneaking around the back lots like this?'

'What are you doing out here?' came the reply.

'I got a friend in the jail and wanted to talk, that's all.'

'Maybe you'd like to get that friend out of jail.'

'Who are you?' Forbes repeated again. 'Is this some kind of a trick to make me admit I'm thinking of breaking the law?'

Again the harsh chuckle, and Forbes narrowed his eyes as he tried to make out details.

'You know me, Trig, and I've been waiting around this one-horse town for several days hoping you'd show up.'

'Keep talking!' Forbes urged.

'Not here! McCall is making his rounds and we don't want him walking up to us. I'd be forced to kill him, and we can do without stirring up too much trouble around here.'

'Who are you?' Forbes demanded in desperation.

'Remember the Butterfield Detective agent when you were operating in Texas?' The chuckle sounded again, a hard, ruthless sound in the shadows. 'I'm Hank Bolden! We did a deal then, and we can do one now.'

'Hank Bolden!' Forbes grappled in his mind for facts from the past, and suddenly a tight grin appeared on his heavy face. 'Yeah, I remember you! You're a double-dealing detective, a thief on the side of the law!'

'Let's not start name-calling,' Bolden retorted. 'We can work out a good deal around here, Forbes. Are you interested?'

'What have you got to offer?'

'Your life for one thing!' The gun that was visible waggled a little. 'I'm working for the railroad right now. One of Chet Manning's men. He left me in town to watch for you showing up. I guess he knows you pretty good, huh?'

'Manning!' Forbes's voice turned harsh. 'How come you work for the railroad?'

'It's the only kind of work I know.'

'But what for you want to make a deal with the likes of me?'

'It worked the last time, didn't it? You got a hatful of dollars and so did I. A peace officer doesn't make a great deal of dough, you know. You guys get most of the gravy.'

Forbes chuckled harshly. 'Yeah! I remember you were always ready to make a fast buck. Okay, Bolden, so what's your pitch now?'

'I got a feeling that there will be plenty of rich pickings from the railroad if Chet Manning lost his seat in the big saddle as troubleshooter! I could mebbe get his job because of my credentials, and with me running things you could strike when and where the dough is, with me feeding you information.'

'What kind of a cut would you expect?' Forbes's eyes were glittering, for this was the kind of deal he needed to set up.

'I'll take a quarter share of everything you pick up and you make sure Chet Manning dies.' Bolden's tone was crisp, filled with determination. 'For some reason Manning didn't cotton to me from the moment he set eyes on me, and I got the feeling that the first thing he'll do when he's got the time is make some inquiries into my past. If he gets in touch with Butterfield they'll tell him everything and I'll be out of a job here. So Manning has got to die.'

'You're talking to a man who wants the same thing,' Forbes retorted. 'And there are a couple of people in the jail who feel the same way! Looks like Chet Manning has made himself a real mess of enemies! Okay, Bolden, you got yourself the makings of a deal. Put away that gun in case it goes off accidentally. We can do business. I got myself a new gang now Yaro is finished.'

'I heard about them!' Bolden chuckled. 'You hit the bank in Gadson Flats and killed the town marshal.'

'That's right!' It was Forbes's turn to grin. 'But before we can make any kind of a deal I want to get those friends of mine out of jail. I need them.'

'That's easy!' Bolden holstered his gun, tightening his lips when Forbes lowered his hands. 'Just remember one thing, Trig. I'm faster on the draw than you are, so don't try to trick me, huh?'

'Not me!' Forbes replied with a throaty chuckle. 'We can make a lot of dough between us. This must be my lucky day. But how can I get my friends out of jail? You don't want me to tackle Barney McCall.'

'That's right!' Bolden reached into his left hip pocket and produced two large keys, tossing them to Forbes, who caught them deftly and held them up to the light coming through the jail window. 'The smaller one opens the front office door and the bigger one opens the cells. You can get your friends out of that jail any time you like. But you'll need to create a diversion to draw McCall to the other end of town before you start anything.'

'Got any ideas?'

'Sure. We got to make a lot of trouble for Manning before he dies. Run him ragged. Make his bosses figure that he ain't up to handling the job, and if I can shine where he fails then it will go good for me. I'll wind up with Manning's job and he'll be dead.'

'I'm listening,' Forbes said eagerly. 'What do I do for a start?'

'Saddle up horses for your friends in the jail, then go down to the railroad depot and set fire to it. While the town turns out to handle the blaze you can walk in here and turn your friends loose. If their horses are tethered out back then they should be able to get away without trouble.'

Forbes's eyes glinted as he considered, then nodded enthusiastically.

'You sure worked that out fine, Bolden. That's slick! If you handle the rest of it like this we won't have anything to worry about.'

'That's right. Now before you go we got to work out how to get in contact with each other. You got friends in this town, I figure.'

'Sure. There's a Cantina down at the other end of the town. Belongs to a Mex called Martinez. Mama Maria works there. I'll tell her you're my friend and she'll collect and pass messages for me. I'll keep in touch with her.'

'Manning has got to find a lot of trouble on the railroad, and when the time is right he's got to die. Remember that.' Bolden spoke in harsh tones. 'If Manning gets word from Butterfield about me then I'm all washed up around here and we'll both miss out on a lot of dough.'

'Don't worry about Manning! He's as good as dead!' Forbes grinned .'Okay, partner! I'll be on my way now!'

'Watch out for McCall,' Bolden warned. 'See you around, Trig. Soon as I get the hang of the way they run the railroad around here I'll be letting you know about gold and money shipments.'

'I'll be waiting!' Forbes turned and faded into the shadows, and, as he lost himself in the darkness, he had an impulse to swing around and blast Hank Bolden where he stood. He looked over his shoulder, his hand moving towards his gun, and was surprised to discover that the ex-detective had already vanished. He shrugged, grinning to himself. He needed Bolden now because the crooked troubleshooter would be able to put him on to the valuable money shipments that frequently travelled the railroad.

Forbes went along to the stable, remaining in the shadows, watching for signs of McCall, and he was very careful until he spotted the town marshal entering a saloon. Checking through a window, he saw McCall having a drink with a tender, and guessed the lawman would stay put for a few minutes. He hurried along to the stable and entered, turning up the lamp hanging from a nail in a post and saddling up a couple of horses. It did not matter to him whose horses he stole, but as he was about to lead both animals out of the stable a man appeared in the open doorway.

'Hey!' he exclaimed. 'What you doing with those two broncs? They ain't yours!'

'I'm saddling them up for a couple of friends,' Forbes rasped. He kept moving forward until he reached the oldster, who confronted him. Although there was suspicion in the stableman's manner he made no attempt to pull the gun holstered on his right hip.

'Who are your friends?' he demanded.

Forbes widened his grin and swung his right fist in a powerful blow. There was a dull thud as his heavy knuckles connected with the old man's jaw, and when the body sagged to the floor, Forbes kicked it viciously, aiming for the head and then the ribs. He led the two horses out into the night, not caring that they stepped upon the motionless figure, and then he swung into the saddle of one animal and led the other as he rode out of town and made a circle to get to the rear of the jail. He tethered the pair of mounts some distance out, then went to check on McCall once more.

The marshal had left the saloon, and Forbes went along the street, grinning when he saw McCall in another saloon. He went on his way, making for the railroad depot, and when he crossed the tracks and lost himself in the deep shadows surrounding the new buildings at the terminus he chuckled hoarsely. This would be fun.

Checking through several smaller buildings, he found what he was looking for. His nose told him that he had found the kerosene store. He picked up a heavy can and moved stealthily through the shadows to the main building, throwing the liquid over the tinder-dry walls, then entering and sousing the floor and contents of some of the rooms. He departed and grabbed a handful of dry grass, twisting it into a torch, lighting it and hurling it into the kerosene soaked room. The next instant the room was a blazing inferno.

Forbes withdrew and made his way across the back lots to the jail, passing along the alley beside it to the main street. He stood in the alley mouth, waiting and watching, his right hand upon the butt of his holstered gun.

The silence was intense, and darkness reigned over the sleeping town. Most of the saloons and bars were now closed, with only a few yellow lights at various windows. Impatience caught at Forbes's anxious mind and he peered along the street in the direction of the depot. There were no ominous signs of fire yet, no smell of smoke or the menacing crackle of flames, and he began to wonder at the success of his undertaking. He shrank back into the shadows as two quiet figures passed along the street, and he grinned as he imagined them spotting the fire and raising the alarm. The next instant a gun crashed three times, sending heavy, sullen echoes across the sleeping town, and Forbes tightened his lips, fearing a trap of some kind until he realised that someone was raising the alarm. A man came running along the street from the direction of the depot, yelling for the marshal, shouting the dreaded word that was feared more than any other in the sun-baked towns of the south-west.

McCall appeared from the shadows opposite, calling to the man, and they met some yards from the alley mouth where Forbes was concealed. He heard their voices, the man's excited warning of the fire, and McCall sent him to sound the fire alarm along the street. The townsman ran to obey and McCall went fast along the sidewalk in the direction of the depot.

Forbes grinned, and his dark eyes glinted as he moved on to the sidewalk, producing the keys Bolden had given him. He knew he would have a few minutes in hand, even if McCall figured the fire was no accident and came running back to guard his jail. There were figures appearing on the street now, and Forbes quickly let himself into the jail, closing the door and moving through the dim light that invaded the office by way of the big front windows. He bumped into the desk and skirted it, cursing viciously and rubbing his left thigh, and eventually found the door that gave access to the cells. He paused for a moment, listening intently, hearing voices out on the street as men went hurrying by in answer to the call of the fire alarm. Then he entered the cell block, moistening his lips as he thought of the woman asleep in one of the cells.

'What's happening out there?' It was Trimble's voice, and Forbes cursed silently as he fought down the urge to kill the man. He would need Trimble to get Glory to safety.

'This is Trig Forbes!' he rasped. 'I'm busting you out of here, so stay quiet and move fast.' He reached Trimble's cell as he spoke, and quickly unlocked the door. 'Where's Glory?'

'Opposite!' There was fear and shock in Trimble's tones. 'Where's the marshal?'

'Forget about him!' Forbes unlocked the door of Glory's cell and entered, bending over the bunk, reaching out a big hand to grab her shoulder. He shook her gently, feeling a pang of

121

emotion as he touched her, but he fought down his urges and shook her awake. 'Come on, Glory,' he said hoarsely. 'It's Forbes, come to take you out of here. Hurry it up before we have trouble.'

Glory gasped but did not speak, and Forbes led the way to the back door, fumbling with the key until the lock turned. Then he led the way across the back lots, hurrying them to where the horses waited.

'Get mounted!' he rasped. 'Hightail it out of here to the hide-out and stay there until I show up. I got a few things to do around here. But we're really in business now. Trimble, I'm holding you responsible for Glory's safety. Don't get picked up again, and this time do as you're told.'

Trimble made no reply, but mounted swiftly, and he was ready to ride before the girl had hit the saddle. Then they rode out and Forbes stood staring after them, his thick lips compressed as he watched the woman's shadowy figure. When they had disappeared into the night he turned and looked at the red glow arising from the fire he had started, and chuckled hoarsely as he went back to the poorer quarter of the town. He entered the cantina by the kitchen door, eyes glinting as he thought of Mama Maria, and pulled up short in the kitchen, for three dusty Mexicans were waiting for him, guns drawn, dark faces alert.

Forbes halted as if he had run into a wall, looking from one hard face to another until he found himself staring at Miguel del Soro. He nodded slowly, his eyes glinting, but made no effort to raise his hands. Miguel del Soro was grinning, his teeth startlingly white, and the big gun in his hand glittered in the lamplight. He was tall and powerfully built, dressed in dusty range clothes, and his huge sombrero hung down his back, suspended by its strap around his throat.

'So the tales I heard about Trig Forbes are true!' he commented in faultless English.

'Seems like I heard a few tales myself which I didn't believe,' Forbes retorted. 'Somebody told me you stole my gal, Soro!'

'Maria is my *senorita*,' the Mexican replied.

'She was my gal first, so I figure you stole her from me!' There was no fear in Forbes, and he ignored the other two men, his dark eyes slitted as he watched the Mexican.

'You want to fight for Maria?' del Soro demanded, holstering his gun. His thin hand remained hovering above the butt and a reckless grin came to his dusty, lean features. His eyes were narrowed and bright.

'Not right now, or here in town at any time,' Forbes replied, fighting his instincts. 'And I don't figure to draw against you with a couple of your men holding guns on me.'

Soro snapped an order in Mexican and the two men holstered their guns but did not relax. Forbes grinned.

'I still ain't fighting it out here,' he said. 'This is the only place in town where I can hide out. You still figuring Mama Maria is your gal, Soro?'

'She is mine!' There was a note of finality in the Mexican's silky voice.

'So you are stealing her from me!' A grin stretched Forbes's lips.

'That is not true, *amigo*. I have taken a fancy to her and I take what I want. I do not steal. I have no desire to break the Gringo law north of the border. I come here to rest up from my side of the border. I am safe here so I wish no trouble. But you are not the man to go away peacefully, my friend!'

'I guess I ain't!' Forbes retorted, and his eyes began to glitter although the grin was still on his lips. 'Mama Maria is my gal and no stinking Mex is gonna take over from me!'

Tension flooded the room, and Forbes's grin widened, for no weapons were in evidence now. He saw del Soro's face change expression, and was ready as the Mexican reached once more for his gun. Forbes made his play, and both heavy Colts leaped into his big hands. He fought down the impulse to start triggering, and covered the trio, stopping their quick movements almost before they had begun.

'That's better!' he grated, and now viciousness began to show in his heavy face. 'Lift your hands, the three of you! You reckoned I was a push-over, Soro, and that's where you made your mistake. Now turn around, all of you. I don't like the look of your ugly faces. Show me your backs, Greasers!'

They turned, their hands raised, and Forbes holstered his left-hand gun and went around them, snaking their weapons out of their holsters, feeling for hidden weapons. He relieved each man of at least one gun and a knife, throwing them into a corner, and then grunted his satisfaction and ordered del Soro to bind his two friends. When they were securely tied and lying on the floor, Forbes holstered his right-hand gun, and now his eyes were blazing with fury, although a grin still clung to his twisted lips.

'So you figured you could steal my gal, and get away with it, and kill me into the bargain, huh?' he demanded. 'Well I got news for you, Soro! I'm gonna twist your head clean off your shoulders with my bare hands. I'll let everyone know that no man lays a hand on Trig Forbes's property and lives long to brag about it.'

He lunged forward then, striking with the speed and power of a cougar. Del Soro tried to evade the big hands that reached for him, but nothing could stop Forbes, and when the Mexican felt the hands take him around the neck he punched with all his strength at Forbes's face and body. But Forbes did not feel the blows. A terrible passion filled him. It was like a red mist dropping before his eyes. He seized the Mexican in a stranglehold, almost lifting del Soro's feet from the floor, and choked the man to death, growling in his throat like a wild animal.

When del Soro fell limply to the floor, Forbes dropped to his knees, holding his death grip until the blinding fury which controlled him began to abate. By degrees his sight and hearing returned and he became aware of his surroundings once more. Sweat poured down his face and his fingers and wrists ached, locked in a relentless grip around the Mexican's neck. With difficulty he broke his hold, releasing the body and pushing himself unsteadily to his feet, to find the two bound Mexicans staring at him with frightened eyes.

Forbes drew a deep breath and left the kitchen, pushing into the private room next door to find Martinez and Mama Maria standing motionless with fear. Their eyes widened at the sight of him, and Martinez crossed himself. He spoke with an effort.

'Senor Forbes! We were afraid for you! Del Soro arrived during your absence and threatened us if we tried to warn you.'

Forbes paused, looking indecisive. There were impulses raging through him, but he knew he needed these people and he drew a heavy breath, grinning tightly as he looked at the frightened Mama Maria.

'What about you, Mama Maria?' he demanded. 'Who do you want, me or del Soro?'

'You, Senor Trig!' she said eagerly. 'But I am afraid of del Soro when you are not around.'

'Uhuh! Well he ain't gonna bother you any more. He's dead!' Martinez cried out in alarm and Forbes grinned.

'Yeah,' he said. 'He's dead in your kitchen, and his two sidekicks are hogtied. You better figure on how to get them out of here so the local law don't get wind of it. I don't want no trouble around here, Martinez! Me and my friends got some more business to handle in Jules Crossing, so earn yourself some extra pesos by getting rid of them Greasers, huh?'

'I will take care of it, Senor Forbes, but it will cost money.' Martinez wrung his hands, his face showing fear.

'Okay. You get the job done then let me know what it costs. I'll shell out.' Forbes grabbed Mama Maria's arm and made for the door. 'Now I'm going back to bed. Half the night is gone and I ain't slept yet!'

'But, Senor Forbes, I may need help,' Martinez said. 'Del Soro has friends in this town and they could make trouble. You will have to be ready for gunplay or knives.'

'Include me out!' Forbes rasped. 'Call me in the morning when my friends show up asking for me. Any other trouble you better handle yourself, Martinez! That's what I pay you for!'

He departed with the woman and went to his room.

Chapter Twelve

Manning and Joe Carver rode for several days, checking three of the hideouts that Manning knew about, but they never set eyes on another human. Each day was an eternity of hot torture under the blazing sun, of peering through slitted eyes into glare that concealed much of their surroundings. The silence that enveloped them, except for their own small sounds of travel, was heavy and stifling. The only other things moving under the brassy sky were a buzzard or two swinging in lazy circles above the serrated ridges.

The country was an enemy, each ridge a personal obstruction to be surmounted, and when one passed another like it lay ahead of them. A man had to know the country to be able to travel it, for it was a land virtually without water, visited only by men on the run, desperate killers who sneaked through it like vicious wolves.

Manning reined up on a skyline and cuffed back his grey stetson, wiping sweat from his forehead as he peered around. Great table-lands reared up solidly against the brilliant sky, creating harsh horizons all around, and here and there lofty pinnacles pointed even higher, as if intent upon escaping the hot, dead heat of the sullen canyons and arroyos.

He glanced to the north, where great peaks pierced the heavens, purpled by distance, remote and majestic. He smiled wryly, his eyes mere slits under the power of the glare, and resolutely dragged his gaze away, looking west and south and trying to forget the shade back there, the water, trees and grass.

Joe Carver had to clear his throat before he could speak, and his tanned face was whitened by dust, his eyes red-rimmed. He peered at Manning, then grinned. They had not spoken for many hours, and now they were muscle-weary from sitting their jolting saddles, burdened by the sun.

'You figure we're gonna have some luck, Chet?' he rasped, the echoes of his speech muffled by the great stillness.

'I guess not!' Manning reached for his canteen, took a sip of lukewarm water, rinsed his mouth, then spat. He dismounted and removed his neckerchief, shaking the dust from it and moistening it before applying it to the velvet nostrils of his mount. The animal whickered a little, its dark eyes rolling as it peered down at him, and he patted the animal, smiling slowly. 'They ain't using any of the hideouts I know about, Joe, and I figure there must be a thousand places around here where they could lie up. An army wouldn't be able to smoke them out.'

'Water is the key to it,' Carver retorted, dismounting and attending to his horse. His shadow was small upon the ground. The sun was almost overhead. The faint breeze that stirred along the ridge was hot as the inside of a furnace. 'If we knew all the water holes we'd have them.'

'I didn't figure this would be anything but a waste of time,' Manning commented, remounting and staring in the direction he planned to ride. 'But we had to check these places out. I reckon Forbes ain't fool enough to use Yaro's old haunts. I figure we better swing south now and hit Gadson Flats. It ain't no more than twenty miles from here. But there's a little spread owned by a man named Turner that we'll drop into on the way to town. I heard a whisper that Turner runs a stop-over for outlaws who are passing through. Maybe he's seen something of Forbes and this new gang.'

'If Turner is a man like that then he won't talk. His kind never do. It ain't worth the risk.'

'We'll take a look around there, anyways,' Manning said.

They rode on, and hour after broiling hour passed. For all the change in the scenery they might not have stirred a yard, but Manning was well aware of their position, and they hit an arroyo and followed it through a great outcrop of copper-coloured rock, emerging later to be faced by a low ridge. When they reached the crest of the ridge they reined up, and Joe Carver uttered a gasp of relief at sight of a creek glinting in the evening sunlight. A cluster of ranch buildings huddled by the flat stretch of water, and Manning caught Carver's eyes and nodded.

'Turner's place,' he said. 'He lives here with his wife and

son. They don't run much in the way of cattle. Horses mostly!'

They rode down the slope and picked their way towards the ranch. When they neared the buildings a couple of riders started towards them, and Manning dropped a hand to the butt of his gun.

'Careful, Joe,' he warned. 'There could be some hardcases around.'

Carver nodded and let his right hand slide towards his hip, but they kept moving, and within a few moments Manning recognised one of the oncoming pair.

'That one on the right is Billy Dainton!' he exclaimed. 'He's a deputy sheriff. Last saw him in Buffalo Junction when I came back to duty. Heard tell over the telegraph that he might be going to Gadson Flats to represent the law after Hart Loman was gunned down!'

The two newcomers reined up, and Manning nodded as he eased himself in the saddle, looking into the youthful face of Billy Dainton.

'Howdy, Billy!' he greeted. 'What you doing this long way out of town?'

The deputy sheriff slowly shook his head as he stared into Manning's hard face. His features seemed pale beneath their tan, his eyes uneasy.

'Figured to look around for signs of Forbes and that new bunch he's riding with!' he said. 'We got here about four hours ago, Chet. Found all the Turners dead! They been murdered!'

Manning tightened his lips, glancing at Carver, who shook his head.

'They been dead long?' Manning demanded.

'About a week, we reckon.' Dainton drew a sharp breath and held it for a moment, his expression showing distaste. 'You figure it could be some of Trig Forbes's work?'

'I don't make guesses in my business, Billy.' Manning shook his head. 'You got any news about happenings around the country?'

'There was trouble in Jules Crossing. Someone burned down your new depot there and, when the panic subsided and the fire was out, Barney McCall discovered that someone had walked into his jail and turned two of his prisoners loose.'

'Glory Harpe and Grat Trimble!' Manning said through clenched teeth.

128

'That's right.' Dainton sighed heavily. 'That's how come I was out this way. I heard tell that Turner took in outlaws on the dodge. I figured I might come across Forbes and the others here.'

'You came out with just one man?' Manning asked. 'Ain't that a mite foolish, Billy?'

'I got six more men at the ranch,' Dainton replied. 'Your new man, Milt Aitken, is in Gadson Flats waiting for you to show up.'

'Yeah, well we're riding there now,' Manning said. 'I reckon we're just wasting our time searching for the gang. This is a hell of a country in which to find people.'

'We're riding back to town ourselves,' Dainton said. 'Be glad to give you some company.'

'Fine! I'm wondering if Bolden was wise to what happened in Jules Crossing! I left him there to keep an eye on things!'

'I wish you'd brought him with you and left me behind,' Carver commented.

Manning was silent as they rode into the ranch, and he looked around intently. When he spotted three fresh mounds of earth across the yard he pulled his lips tight, shaking his head a little. Three people murdered, had been dead a week, and Forbes was loose in the territory. He recalled that Hank Bolden had said Forbes was a maniac where women were concerned and, as he dismounted, he caught Billy Dainton's eye.

'Billy, how did these people die?' he demanded.

'Turner was strangled. We found him lying in the barn. His face was black and his tongue hung out. Whoever took him by the neck sure meant to do him in. Chad Turner was lying in the corral, face down in the dust. He was knifed.'

'And the woman?' Manning asked softly.

'Shot once in the breast.' Dainton's thin tone was unsteady. 'In the kitchen. She must have died immediately.'

'Were there any signs that she had been raped?'

Dainton seemed to turn even more pale as he paused before replying. Then shook his head.

'I couldn't say, Chet. She was in her night clothes, wearing a dressing gown. She'd been dead almost a week, I guess. We just put those poor people in their graves as soon as we could.'

Manning nodded as he turned slowly to gaze around at the ranch and its perimeter. It was impossible to be sure that Trig

9   129

Forbes had been here. Any drifter with murderous tendencies could have dropped in and taken the family unawares, and there were many such desperate men in the country.

'So Jules Crossing was hit!' he said half to himself. 'I figure no one but Forbes would bust Glory and Trimble out of jail!' His eyes narrowed as he considered the wasted days they had spent searching for signs of the outlaws. 'Joe, you ride back to Gadson Flats with Billy and the posse. Make contact with Milt Aitken and take a train to Jules Crossing. See what you can pick up about the trouble there. If there is anything to work on get at it. But before you leave Gadson Flats send a wire to Asa Blaine in Buffalo Junction, huh?'

'Sure, Chet.'

'Tell him what we've done so far. Ask him to run a check on Hank Bolden for me. I want to know all about his past activities. Check with the Butterfield Detective Agency in Fort Worth.'

'Okay. But what are you planning to do now?'

'I'm going to circle north and east, checking a few more likely places on my way back to Jules Crossing,' Manning decided. 'I'm not forgetting that Trimble was a freighter in this country for a number of years. He'll know the area like an Injun. He'll have a lot of friends around, and I know some of them. If nothing crops up then I'll be in Jules Crossing in a few days. We'll meet up there. But I need to get this business settled so we can get back to real railroad work.'

'Right.' Carver nodded. 'Do we have time to stock up here before riding on?'

'I'll be heading back to Gadson Flats in about thirty minutes,' Billy Dainton said. 'A couple of my men are cooking some grub and you're welcome to share what we got.'

'I'll take some supplies and top up my canteen,' Manning said. 'I want to get moving. If Glory and Trimble headed out the way I figure they would, then I got a pretty good idea where they might be, within a few miles.'

'You'll have to watch out for Forbes,' Carver warned. 'If he's the kind of man Bolden says he is then he won't let Glory Harpe get too far away from him.'

'That's right!' Manning grinned tightly. 'I'm hoping she will draw Forbes.'

Carver gazed into Manning's face and pulled his lips tight when he saw the expression showing there. He nodded slowly. 'I can understand how you feel,' he said. 'If it wasn't for these rogues we'd be having a quiet time of it. They obviously ain't got trouble at end of track or we'd have heard about it. I guess they're still pushing the rails west.'

They went into the ranch, and Manning sensed a grim atmosphere, an intangible smell of death about the place. He wrinkled his nose, recalling the awful smell of decomposing flesh in the undertaker's in Gadson Flats, and suddenly his stomach heaved and he felt nauseous. But he fought it down and controlled it, clenching his teeth. He needed a good meal. He had to maintain his strength for the arduous days still ahead, and when he thought of the people he wanted to catch his mind steeled itself. There was a great deal of trouble looming for the railroad if he did not get Forbes and the others.

The sun was well over in the western half of the sky when they rode out of the deathly still ranch, and Manning accompanied the posse until they had passed out of sight of the buildings. Then he took his leave, riding away in a half circle, moving back for another glimpse of the Turner place. He left his horse in cover and took his Winchester, bellying down atop a ridge to lie in patient vigil. He did not move until the sun went down and gloom began to steal into the low places. If Glory and Trimble had travelled in this direction then they might be in this area. Trimble would know the Turners offered sanctuary to men on the dodge, and it was quite possible he would bring Glory here.

Full darkness came slowly, and Manning lay motionless in his position, relieved with the lessening of heat that had tortured him all day. The breeze that came gently over the ridge was warm, but the fire had gone and he breathed deeply as he waited. He would remain here until around midnight, resting and watching, and if his quarry had not appeared by then he would push on at an angle towards Jules Crossing, hoping to come across signs of Glory and Trimble.

An hour passed and Manning felt his eyelids grow heavy. Living rough for days at a time took its toll of alertness and strength, and he knew he would have to sleep for an hour or two before making another sustained effort. He let his head fall upon his arms, but his ears were keened for sound and he

131

knew he could pick up steel-shod hoofs on hard ground over a great distance.

When he heard what he was listening for he raised his head, his features tightening into a grim expression. A hoof had clicked against a stone. He peered into the shadows, making out the shapeless black mass of the house, and detected a faint movement, nothing more than the displacement of shadow patterns, approaching the yard. He moistened his lips and prepared to move in on foot, easing himself over the crest of the ridge and picking his way down the slope to the fence that marked the perimeter of the yard. The breeze was in his face, carrying with it the furtive sounds of someone approaching the ranch.

Reaching the fence, Manning dropped to one knee and took a long, careful look around. He saw a rider sitting his mount in the gateway, obviously checking out the place, and his lips tightened a little as he peered around for the presence of others. But this newcomer seemed to be alone.

Manning eased his sixgun from its holster and gripped it in his right hand. He was conscious of his fear of making a mistake, and realised how desperately he needed to start a clean-up. If he failed to pull in Forbes and his new bunch quickly then the badman would begin to make himself a reputation, and the longer he remained free the harder it would be for anyone to capture him.

The rider was now dismounting, and Manning remained in cover, more concerned at the moment about possible friends of this rider. He did not move a muscle as the figure left its horse and sneaked forward to the house, losing himself in its shadow, and the silence pressed in closely while the wind blew free.

Minutes passed before the figure suddenly reappeared. It paused beside the waiting horse and whistled, the sound cutting through the night. Manning drew a steady breath as he waited, and moments later heard a hoof striking rock then the creak of saddle leather. He narrowed his eyes, turning his head slowly to pick up movement, and spotted a second rider coming in. The two merged into one and Manning waited it out, not daring to move for fear of attracting attention. The second rider dismounted, and Manning figured he could hear their undertones as they conversed. His patience was firm as he awaited developments.

The second newcomer went into the house, and Manning flattened himself slightly, trying to get the figure in silhouette, but the house was beyond it and he could not form an outline. He watched the other rider, and the man led the two horses across the yard to a water trough. When the animals had taken water they were led into the barn opposite.

A dim yellow light pierced the gloom surrounding the barn, and Manning eased upright and started across the yard, intent upon getting a glimpse of the man. He reached the wall of the barn, found a convenient knot-hole, and applied his right eye to the small aperture. His teeth clicked together when he recognised the man forking hay into the stalls where he had put the two horses. It was Grat Trimble.

Manning grinned as he drew back. He holstered his sixgun and held his rifle steady. The other figure would be Glory, he guessed instantly, and moved around to enter the barn. He could deal with some of his problems now. But he hesitated. Who had busted them out of the Jules Crossing jail? It could only have been Trig Forbes. Manning accepted that. He also knew Trimble and Glory would not talk. He had failed to get information from them, and badly needed to come up with Forbes. It seemed obvious that these two could lead him right into the outlaw hideout.

He knew he was not running much risk by not recapturing these two immediately. While he was watching them they could not shoot him in the back, and if they led him to Forbes then he could overlook their freedom in exchange for the outlaw.

Moving quietly, he went back to the crest of the ridge and prepared his horse for travel, taking it to another spot where it was more convenient. Then he went back to watch and stayed motionless and silent through the next four hours while Trimble and the woman remained in the house. He dozed at times, but with one eye open, starting up immediately any unnatural sound reached him. The sky to the east was greying with approaching dawn when he stirred and readied himself to move out. He had barely straightened when he saw Trimble leaving the house to go into the barn. Minutes later the man reappeared leading two horses, and he watered them at the trough before going on to the porch of the house. The front door opened and a woman's figure appeared, carrying a heavy gunny sack

133

and two canteens. The sky was turning crimson over in the east and daylight was not far away.

Manning watched until the two had mounted and started away from the ranch. Then he went to his own horse and tightened the cinch, stepping up into the saddle and riding out, prepared for a long, hot day trailing his quarry. He rode easily, but maintained sharp vigilance. There was no sign of Forbes around, but he figured the big outlaw would be showing up again. Glory was the bait! Manning was aware of the fact, and grinned to himself as he figured that the badman's weakness would catch him out.

He soon became aware that the two were not making for some remote hideout. They were circling slightly to move towards Buffalo Junction and Manning thrust out his underlip as he tried to guess at their destination. Were they going to look for him or were they on their way to rendezvous with Trig Forbes and the new gang?

Three days passed and they covered hot, dusty miles. Manning soon discovered that Trimble was taking no chances. The man kept glancing around as if he feared pursuit. But Glory seemed glued to her saddle and barely eased her muscles as the time passed. Manning did not trail from behind them but moved out to their right rear quarter, staying behind ridges and other cover, watching them from time to time in order to judge their general direction. He chewed dry food in the saddle and swigged water sparingly from his canteen. He was hot and dusty, stubbled and gaunt, but there was no relaxing of his determination, and eagerness bubbled in the back of his mind. At last he was making progress.

During the fourth afternoon he eased forward, gaining upon his quarry, knowing they were not far from Buffalo Junction but angling away from the town, and he realised that they had a different destination. When he reined up behind a ridge and dismounted to watch his two guides he bellied down on the crest and found himself staring down at a stretch of railroad track. His lips tightened. This was the new track being pushed towards Apache Pass!

Trimble turned left when he reached the track and led the girl alongside it. Manning mounted and followed, remaining behind the ridge, and he nodded to himself when Trimble paused at a deep gully that was spanned by a wooden trestle bridge. Now he understood. They were going to do something to the track. Their hatred was such that they were prepared to strike at the railroad the easiest way possible, and he dismounted and took his rifle as he moved forward to investigate.

Glory was leading the horses into cover behind some rocks near the track and Trimble was on one knee, working on a package he had taken from a saddlebag. Manning narrowed his eyes as he tried to make out details, but he was more than sixty yards from the track and could not see until Trimble straightened and turned to go to the trestle bridge. Then he saw what he imagined to be sticks of dynamite in Trimble's hands, and there were fuses attached to them.

So that was it! Manning's teeth clicked together, but he hesitated only for a moment. He needed these two to lead him to Trig Forbes and he was prepared to pay a high price for the opportunity of catching up with the outlaw.

Snaking forward, he moved from rock to rock, closing in upon the girl, aware that he had to disarm her before getting to grips with Trimble. He saw the ex-freighter climbing out along the trestle, moving slowly, making for the very centre of the span.

Glory was intent upon watching Trimble's progress, and Manning moved in behind her, using all his craft. But one of the horses sensed his presence and whickered softly, an unmistakeable warning to anyone who knew horses. Glory swung around immediately, coming face to face with Manning, who was a dozen feet behind her.

The woman's mouth gaped in shock, but her reflexes were good. She was wearing a holstered sixgun and her right hand dropped to its butt. Manning opened his mouth to call a warning, but the girl was fast, and before he could utter a word she was clearing leather with her .38, canting the muzzle to bring it into line with him. He cursed, sweating as he threw himself at her, swinging the rifle as he moved, and the muzzle struck the sixshooter, knocking it out of her hand. As it flew through the air in a high arc, Manning hit her on the jaw with his left fist, felling her instantly.

He knew she would not surrender. He had to take her, kill her if necessary, and that was one of the grim facts of his job. He was ready to make war on a woman if it meant saving the railroad.

Chapter Thirteen

Trig Forbes was awakened early the next morning by Martinez knocking on the bedroom door. He grunted and kicked Mama Maria out of the bed, then yelled for silence.

'But Senor Trig!' Martinez called through the panels. 'There is a lawman down here to see you. He says it is important.'

Forbes sprang out of bed and grabbed his guns as panic exploded in his mind. Then he caught his breath and wondered if it could be Hank Bolden.

'What does he look like, Martinez?' he snarled, aware that if it were Barney McCall the lawman would have rushed the room with guns drawn. When the Mexican described Bolden, Forbes sighed in relief. 'He ain't a damn lawman, but show him up, okay?' He turned to get dressed, glaring at Mama Maria. 'Get out of here. I don't want anyone to see you.'

The woman hurriedly gathered her clothes and departed, and Forbes was sitting on the bed pulling on his riding boots when Bolden came into the room. The troubleshooter paused and looked around, then came to confront Forbes.

'You got the prisoners away all right,' he commented. 'I'm taking a big chance coming here to see you but I got something important to talk over. I let you get your jailbreak handled right as proof of my good intentions, and now you know I'm on the level with you, Trig, we can get down to real business.'

'What's that?' Forbes eyed Bolden suspiciously. 'The deal we talked about last night still holds good, huh? You'll feed us information about gold shipments?'

'That's right, and you'll kill Chet Manning. But I also work for Western Pacific, Trig. That's why I'm on the inside with the S & W. Western Pacific figures that Ben Yaro and thirty gunhands was the wrong way to handle the S & W. What they want is a small group of about half a dozen men who can

136

lose themselves in the wilderness when they're not hitting the railroad. You're gonna lead that bunch, Trig, and you're gonna start right now. I don't know if you've got the rights of the set-up between the two railroad companies, but it ain't the first one to reach Apache Pass who will get the contracts for the entire south-west. It's the first one to run a train to the entrance to the pass who wins. Bear that in mind. What you've got to do is blow up trestle bridges and block the tracks the S & W are putting down. I know you're a skilled man with explosives. You've blown open enough bank safes in your time. Well there's a blasting powder store on the back lots behind the general store here in town. Get a pack horse and load it with whatever explosives and other gear you'll need. Then get to hell out and hit that new track the S & W are pushing towards Apache Pass. Do the job right and you'll stop their progress for six months. Western Pacific needs a few weeks to get their heads in front. Can I trust you to do that?'

'Sure. I told Yaro it was the way to handle it but he wouldn't listen to me. But what about our deal? We need to grab some dough.'

'There'll be a big pay-off if you stop the S & W in their tracks. After that you can begin to hit the express cars for what they're carrying, and with Manning dead I should be able to take over his job. Handle this right, Trig, and we'll both wind up filthy rich.'

'I'll get moving right away. I've got three good men to side me. They were part of Squint Delmont's gang before Manning chewed them up. They hate Manning's guts so they'll go along with me. And there's Yaro's woman and Grat Trimble. They're the two who will get Manning for us. I'll head out right away and start operating.'

'I'm relying on you, but Manning must go pretty quick. He doesn't like me, and if he checks on me I'll be out of a job. Now I've got to get out of here. I'll be listening for reports of trouble on the track, and I mean big trouble.'

'One thing I like doing is raising hell,' Forbes said cheerfully. 'You got yourself a good partner, Bolden.'

The troubleshooter nodded and departed, and Forbes finished dressing, yelling for Mama Maria to get him some breakfast. When he went down into the kitchen he found Hemp Arrel there.

'We got to get to hell out of here, Trig,' the outlaw growled. 'I just come from the stable. There are some dead Mexes in the loft. If we don't get out before they're found the law will think we did it.'

'Saddle up, and get my hoss,' Forbes ordered. 'I got to have me a bite to eat. We're riding out anyway, and we got a big job to do. I'll tell you all about it. And we'll need a pack horse. I'll come along to the back lots behind the general store in about ten minutes. Okay?'

Arrel did not pause to argue. He hurried away, and Forbes grunted his satisfaction as he sat down and began to eat quickly. The sun was barely above the horizon when he finally took his leave of Martinez and Mama Maria, but the Mexican grasped his arm.

'You will pay me for the removal of those dead Mexicans, senor?' he demanded. 'It cost me many pesos to put them out of sight.'

'What, in the loft of the livery barn? You should have done better than that.' Forbes scowled but reached into a breast pocket. He produced a thick roll of bills and peeled some off without counting them, thrusting them into Martinez's ready hand. 'Now you listen to me, Martinez,' he growled. 'In future you keep Mama Maria hog-tied a little, huh? Don't let anyone else go stamping around her while I'm gone. If I come back and find her tangled up with some other guy then there'll be bad trouble for you, and I don't mean maybe.'

'I understand, senor. Don't worry! I will take care of your interests.'

Forbes grunted and departed, making for the back lots, and he saw Arrel and the other two outlaws waiting behind the explosives store, which was well away from all other buildings. He waved to attract their attention, and Arrel rode towards him, leading Forbes's horse. Forbes swung into his saddle and rode back, grinning at the warnings painted on the shack in letters a foot high. He dismounted and used the barrel of one of his Colts to wrench the lock off the door, then looked inside, selecting what he needed. The others loaded the explosives and boxes containing caps, detonators and fuse wire on to the pack horse, and Forbes motioned for them to ride out.

'I'm gonna cut a long fuse and blow up this place,' he explained. 'Then no one will know what's missing. If word got out that someone had busted in here and stolen some gear then the railroad would expect trouble.'

'I don't like it,' Arrel said doubtfully, 'but make sure you give us plenty of time to get clear, huh? We don't want a posse out after us so we have to ride hard with a pack horse loaded with that stuff.'

'I can handle it,' Forbes said, and set to work while they departed. He lit the fuse after laying it carefully, then galloped after the others. They were in a gully leading away from the town when the explosion came – a terrific thunderclap that sent shock waves through the ground. Their horses were scared, but they continued, and Forbes dropped back to ensure that they were not being pursued.

As they continued he explained the situation to the others, and saw satisfaction and greed in their expressions.

'You just do like I tell you and we've got nothing to worry about,' he said proudly. 'We'll clean up around here, and when Manning is dead and our man gets into power we'll be riding an easy trail. But now we got a lot of riding to do without being seen. I want to reach the new track on the south-west side of Buffalo Junction. Set your minds to it and let's ride.'

The others did not reply, and they started the long ride, Forbes taking them across the wilderness with the instincts of a homing pigeon. Days passed and they continued, riding steadily as if they had all the time in the world, but making good speed and saving their horses in case of emergency. But they avoided all frequented places and rode across hard ground where possible. There might be posses out, Forbes assumed, and he would take no chances now.

When they bypassed Buffalo Junction, Forbes felt that he was on home range, and they eventually hit the railroad track they were seeking. They followed it, keeping out of sight in case anyone riding a passing train spotted them and reported their presence. They saw a work train making its routine run, and when Arrel suggested blowing a bridge which they saw, Forbes shook his head.

'We need to get nearer to the end of the track,' he said. 'I got a pretty good idea how to handle this. We've seen three work trains so far, and none of them have been pulling a boxcar loaded with explosives.'

'Ain't we got enough with us?' Arrel demanded, and Santor

139

and Dillon muttered between themselves.

'Sure we have. But I got a plan that will stop the S & W in their tracks. It's the end of the track I want to hit, like Yaro did. That'll cost them plenty.'

'We can't ride in there, and we ain't got a thousand head of cattle to help us,' Snap Dillon commented.

'Nope.' Forbes chuckled. 'We got something better. Just you wait.'

They continued riding, and twice had to duck into cover when they sighted patrols riding the length of the tracks. It was obvious that the S & W had no intention of being caught again, and Arrel complained about the situation.

'If you ask me, Trig, they know that somebody might try something. We ain't gonna be able to get away with this.'

'We expect to take some risk for the money at stake,' Forbes retorted. 'Leave it to me. I ain't likely to make a mistake.'

'I don't like this, Trig,' Ben Santor commented, and Forbes looked at him, his eyes filled with puzzlement.

'What don't you like about it?' he demanded. 'It's money we're after, huh? Well plenty is coming our way if you do like I tell you.'

'I don't see no percentage in hitting the railroad. All we're gonna do is stir up them troubleshooters and have them after our blood. Before we know it we'll be looking into the muzzle of Chet Manning's gun.'

'That's the whole idea of it,' Forbes said in a heavy tone. 'We've got to kill Manning. We ain't got time to look up Glory Harpe and Trimble and set them to the task. It's a chore we've got to handle ourselves. Four of us should be good enough for Manning. Once he's out of the way Hank Bolden will step into the chief troubleshooter's boots and we'll have a clear trail to everything that's shipped on the railroad in these parts.'

'Banks hold money that can't be traced,' Snap Dillon cut in, easing himself in his saddle.

'Yeah, and before you're clear of any town with their money you've got a posse on your heels, ready to cut you down should you fall off your horses. Listen, we've got a contract with Hank Bolden and we're gonna do it. We'll make more dough than you can hope to spend.'

'That's an impossibility,' Santor said with a grin.

'Well, enough for you to grab yourselves a good time some

place where you ain't known,' Forbes retorted. 'Now get the hosses out of here. We're skylined, and if a train passes we'll be spotted. Just remember this. If we do get our sights on Manning I want him taken alive.'

'Alive!' Arrel frowned as he met Forbes's harsh gaze. 'What you got in mind, Trig?'

'I want to make Manning into a fancy-wrapped gift for a friend of mine.' Forbes chuckled. 'Glory Harpe wants him for killing Yaro, and I reckon it would be quite a sight, watching her cutting him up into little pieces.'

'What do we have to tie in with that crazy woman for?' Santor demanded. 'We might have to travel far and fast, Trig, and she would slow us down some.'

'She's personal!' Forbes's eyes gleamed. 'Don't ever forget that she's my property, boys.'

'Does she know that?' Arrel demanded, and Forbes's grin widened.

'Not yet,' he declared. 'I guess it's gonna be fun making her realise it.' He fought down his emotions and wiped sweat from his forehead. 'I figure we can now start shooting up any trains we meet. If we don't start playing hell along this railroad then Manning ain't gonna come after us.'

'But you reckoned we shouldn't blow the tracks, and that's the easiest way of causing trouble.' Arrel shook his head.

'If we blow the tracks they can't send along the boxcars I want to get my hands on,' Forbes explained. 'Just do like I say and leave the planning to me, huh?' He shook loose his rope, which was coiled on his saddlehorn, and pointed to the telegraph poles beside the track. 'I reckon we could start with those, huh? If they find they got no contact with Buffalo Junction they're gonna send someone to find out why. So let's go to work, and we'll be ready for anything.'

Arrel's expression seemed to indicate that he was not in favour of the tactics but he said nothing and they continued towards end of track, following the gleaming rails, lassoing telegraph poles and uprooting them, snapping the singing wires and breaking all contact between Buffalo Junction and end of track.

'That should set the bees abuzzing,' Forbes said at length, standing up in his stirrups and making the saddle leather protest noisily at his weight. 'If my eyes don't deceive me

141

there's a train coming this way right now!' he exclaimed.

Arrel nodded after peering ahead. 'Yeah, that's a train,' he agreed. 'We better move back if we're gonna shoot it up. Passengers have a nasty habit of returning fire! They've had plenty of practice with Indian attacks.'

They moved away from the track, dismounting some fifty yards out and dropping into a gully, dragging their rifles from their saddleboots. Forbes bellied up to the top of the gully and watched the train coming at a fast clip along the track, a column of black smoke spouting from the pot-bellied stack.

'Hey, work 'em over real good,' he shouted joyfully.

The train was a freight, the locomotive pulling loaded flat-cars and a caboose. Forbes started shooting while it was still a long way off, and his bullets struck the locomotive, the flat echoes of his shots cracking like whiplashes. He saw the head and shoulders of the fireman and drew a bead on the target, swinging his rifle to allow for the motion of the train. When he fired, the man on the footplate jerked and disappeared instantly, and Forbes bellowed with laughter.

Then the train was passing in front of them, and four rifles cracked rapidly, spraying the engine with slugs. When the shooting ceased and the train continued along the track, smoke spurting skywards, the click click of the wheels on the rails echoed on the heels of the shots.

'That does it!' Forbes rasped. 'We did a good job. Let's keep riding. I want to be around when Chet Manning comes to check out the trouble. Then we'll really be in business.'

They rode on, following the track at a distance, wary and ready for trouble, and two hours later they spotted an engine pulling a flatcar coming from Buffalo Junction. The flatcar was crowded with men, and Forbes pinched his lips as he counted them.

'More than a dozen,' he commented. 'You figure we can do something about them before they can get into action?'

'The odds ain't no more than four to one against us,' Arrel retorted, grinning. 'They don't have hosses neither. We can always pull out if it gets too hot for us. You want to hit the railroad, don't you?'

'Sure do!' Forbes leaped from his saddle and led his horse behind some rocks. The others followed him, trailing their reins, and they moved back and dropped into firing positions.

The train was puffing black smoke, the snort and pant of the engine sounding clearly across the bright countryside. 'Let 'em have it!' Forbes yelled, and began firing into the thick of the men clustered on the flatcar.

Once again the afternoon was shattered by the angry crack of rapidly firing rifles, and Forbes's dark eyes glistened when he saw men falling off the car as slugs struck them. But there was an almost immediate reply, and spurts of dust leaped up around them.

Forbes emptied his rifle into the men on the car then ducked and reloaded, his face covered with a sheen of sweat. His pulses raced to the thrill of killing, and he swung back into action as quickly as he could. The train did not stop, and they exchanged fire with the surviving railroaders until it was out of range.

When he was mounted, Forbes rode towards the track, followed by the others, and he checked the men who had fallen off the train. Two of the five were still breathing and Forbes dismounted and shot them through the head. He searched the bodies, taking anything of value, then they continued, riding steadily, alert for trouble. Forbes was flushed with success, and kept chuckling to himself as he relived the tense moments of action. He had always seen himself as a gang leader and considered himself better suited to the task than his old boss. Now he had the opportunity to prove it.

Chapter Fourteen

Glory lay unconscious at Manning's feet, and he crouched a little, looking now at Trimble, who was still climbing out on the trestle. He kicked a rifle away from the woman, and looked around to see where her sixgun had fallen. It was well out of her reach and he dropped to one knee at her side, raising an eyelid to check her condition. She was unconscious, but he knew she would not be out longer than a few minutes. He arose and fired a shot in the air, watching Trimble as the crack hammered and sent echoes fleeing to the horizon.

Trimble halted immediately and turned to peer down. He froze when he saw Manning, and remained motionless, unable to believe his eyes. Manning raised the rifle to his shoulder and took aim. There was about fifty yards between them.

'Okay, Trimble, come down nice and easy, and be careful with that explosive.' Manning's voice echoed, and Glory moaned and began to stir. Trimble breathed harshly, still unable to believe what he saw, but the sight of Manning's ominous figure brought fear and anger clashing together in his mind.

'Where in hell did you come from?' he demanded.

'Never mind that. I've been trailing you since you left the Turner ranch. Come down or I'll put a bullet through you.'

'You wouldn't dare.' Trimble's voice was taut with tension. 'I got this dynamite from Turner's ranch, and I'll use it. You better put down your guns before I make a big bang.'

Manning fired the Winchester, splintering a beam close to Trimble's head, and he grinned when the older man ducked. He waited until the echoes of the shot had faded before shouting once more.

'Come on down. There's no other way out for you. I don't scare at all. If you want to blow yourself up then go ahead and do it.'

Fury burst into Trimble's hatred-warped mind and he cursed, pulling the sixgun he had holstered on his right hip. He triggered the big weapon, but spurts of dust in front of Manning warned that he was out of effective pistol-shot. Manning fired again, his bullet clipping a beam within six inches of Trimble's head.

'This is your last warning, Trimble,' he shouted. 'You've had your fun. Now you better come down or my next shot will be through your thick head.'

Trimble set his teeth into his bottom lip, trembling with fury. He was beaten and he knew it. The prospect of jail for a countless number of years was now very real, for he could not count on Trig Forbes springing him yet again. He stared at Manning's figure, so small from his great height, then glanced down at the explosives in his hand. Something snapped in his mind and he cursed at the top of his voice. But he began climbing down the trestle, moving nimbly for a man of his age.

Manning watched intently, and when Trimble reached the ground and began to come towards him, he called a warning.

'Get rid of that explosive, Trimble. Put it down on the ground.'

'You don't want it too near the trestle, do you?' Trimble countered, still coming forward, and his face was set in a harsh expression, his eyes glittering, fixed in a hawk-like stare at Manning. When he drew closer, Manning menaced him with the rifle but nothing was going to stop Trimble. He came forward, intent upon getting to close quarters, and Manning suddenly realised what was in the man's mind.

'Stay put,' he snapped. 'Hold it right there, Trimble.'

'I ain't gonna go back to jail. I'd rather die here and now, and I'm gonna take you with me, Manning.' As he spoke, Trimble lit the fuse which stuck out of the centre of the demolition charge he had prepared. He was twenty yards from Manning, and started running forward, determined to get close.

Manning fired instantly, hitting Trimble in the right thigh, causing him to cartwheel, and smoke drifted from the burning fuse. Trimble tried to get up, dragging his right leg in a shambling run towards Manning, who fired again, his teeth clenched and his eyes slitted. He saw blood spurt from Trimble's shirt front, and the ex-freighter went down again, rolling over and over on the hard ground. Manning looked for cover, and bent to grasp Glory, heaving her across his shoulder. Then he ran for the nearest rocks, hurling himself and the woman behind their cover.

A terrific explosion erupted, but Trimble did not hear it. He was still clutching the explosives, and saw the beginning of a brightness more powerful than the sun. Then blackness swooped and he knew no more. Manning opened his mouth, hands clapped to his ears. Even so he was stunned by the detonation and lay with singing ears for several minutes before he could recover his battered senses. Then he arose, grabbing his rifle, to look for Trimble. He saw a hole in the sun-baked ground and there were shreds of Trimble's clothing lying around to a great distance. A pillar of black smoke was curling skywards, and the intolerable thunder echoed and re-echoed. He swallowed to relieve the pressure in his ears, then heaved a long sigh of thankfulness. The trestle bridge was undamaged.

A movement attracted his attention and he looked around to see Glory trying to sit up. He gulped, irritated by the singing in his ears, and went to stand over her, his rifle in his hands. She gazed up at him with hatred in her eyes.

'You!' she snapped. 'Always you. Where did you come from? Where's Trimble?'

He told her unemotionally, and saw nothing in her expression. She waited until he fell silent, then drew a quick breath.

'I won't rest until you're dead and in your grave,' she said fiercely. 'I'll die trying to get you.'

'Trimble just did that. It's up to you how you go, Glory, but as far as I'm concerned you're going to jail. We're starting towards Buffalo Junction.'

He helped her to her feet and she tried to snatch his sixgun from its holster. He slapped her face hard, then thrust her to the ground.

'I've got a mighty strong notion to teach you some manners,' he rasped. 'You've got it in for me because I killed Yaro in a fair fight. But the last time I saw you, by the creek outside Buffalo Junction, you were making love to me while two of Yaro's gunnies came sneaking up on me. As I recall it, we never did get that love-making finished. I reckon right now would be a pretty good time to end it once and for all.'

'Even you wouldn't do that,' she retorted.

146

He grinned as he put down his rifle and unbuckled his six-gun. 'Oh no? I never turned down a chance in my life, and you sure owe me something.' He placed his weapons out of reach, grasping her by the shoulder and dropping down beside her. She kicked at him and struggled, but he held her as if she were a child, and opened her shirt, revealing her well-rounded breasts. 'I ain't forgetting that you gave yourself to me just to get me naked and helpless. That's about as bad as what I'm gonna do to you. I need sex like a sick man needs medicine. That's all it means to me most of the time. It's an animal-act, that's all, and you're convenient, Glory.'

He began to strip her, warning her to lie quiescent or he would rip her clothes, and when she was bare he gazed with glittering eyes upon her nakedness. She was breathing heavily, her face pale, but she was defiant, and half-wished that Trig Forbes could appear at this very moment. But she would have her revenge, and she summoned up the patience needed.

Manning took her roughly, thrusting himself into her with no thought for her feelings. After days in the saddle he was dirty, sweating, and ready for a woman. He was like an animal, lunging frenziedly at her, his fingers twisting at her breasts and buttocks. She tried to keep him away but his strength was overwhelming and he churned against her, grinding and jerking passionately, driving his manhood ever deeper, plunging in mentally as well as physically, until he climaxed powerfully and gripped her with all his strength. Then he slumped upon her and she lay motionless, imprisoned by his body.

When he had recovered from his exertions he permitted her to dress, and buckled his gunbelt around his waist, tying down the holster. Then he led her to the horses.

'I won't tie you, Glory, but don't make the mistake of trying to get away from me. I'll shoot you if I have to.'

'You're a big man!' she jeered. 'I'd just like to see you up against Trig Forbes, that's all!'

'You could,' he retorted with a glitter in his eyes. 'All you have to do is tell me where he is. I want to meet him!'

'No chance!' She climbed into her saddle. 'I don't know where he is!'

'Perhaps not, but he told you where to go and wait for him, huh?' Manning mounted Trimble's horse and reached for the girl's reins, tying the ends and looping them around his saddlehorn. He gigged the horse and rode on to where his own mount was waiting. As he swung into his own saddle he looked at the woman, meeting her hard gaze, and she laughed harshly, her eyes burning in her ashen face. 'What about it?' he pressed. 'If you want to see me try conclusions with Forbes then show me the way to his hideout. I'll ride in there with you and you'll have a front seat at the showdown.'

'Trig will get word about me being in jail again, and nothing will stop him busting me out. He likes me, Manning, and he's a better man than you've ever been.'

'Get wise to Forbes and the kind of man he is,' he snapped in a flinty tone. 'You spent a night at the Turner spread. Turner used to let outlaws and men on the dodge stop over at his place. But Forbes rode in there and left Turner and his wife and son dead, all murdered. That's the kind of man Trig Forbes is. That's what you are getting yourself mixed up in, Glory!'

She stared at him, her eyes livid, and Manning could see the hatred that was eating at her inside. He shook his head as he rode beside the track towards Buffalo Junction, following the twin rails that glittered in the afternoon sunlight.

When a train appeared in the distance, coming from Buffalo Junction, Manning rode on to the track and stood up in his stirrups, waving his stetson. The engineer sounded the whistle as an indication that he had seen him. Riding to one side, he waited for the engine to arrive, and saw that it was pulling a flatcar and a box car. There were a dozen men on the flatcar, all standing up as the train halted, covering him and Glory with their guns.

Manning was surprised to see Billy Dainton amongst the men, and half a dozen voices started talking when he asked what was going on.

'Hold it!' Manning snapped. 'Billy, what's wrong?'

'We don't know, Chet!' the deputy retorted excitedly, his youthful face flushed with anticipation. 'I got word that a message had been tapped out over the wire asking for help to be sent to end of track. A work train went out earlier because it was reported the telegraph line was down. Someone on that train must have sent the call for help.'

'Okay,' Manning nodded. 'You've got your horses in that box car, I assume.'

'That's right! We don't know what to expect, but we're ready for anything,' Dainton replied.

'Good. Give me a hand to get my prisoner aboard, Billy. She's Glory Harpe.'

'So you got her!' Dainton grinned as he nodded. 'I figure you would if anyone could. But what about Trimble?'

'Dead. I'll tell you about it later!' Manning moved towards the engine. 'Have our horses put into the car, Billy, then we'll roll. 'I'm going with you.'

The deputy nodded and rapped orders to the possemen and, as Manning went to the cab of the locomotive, some of the men jumped off the car and grabbed the three horses. Glory was helped on to the car.

Manning looked at the cars. A ramp had been lowered on the box car and the horses were being loaded. Billy Dainton was crouching beside Glory. Manning nodded slowly, his eyes calculating.

When the train moved on, Manning remained upon the footplate, peering over the engineer's shoulder to see through his window, watching the track far ahead. It was then a fusillade of shots rang out, and slugs struck the metal parts of the loco-motive and screeched agonisingly in ricochet.

Manning spun around, catching a glimpse of gunsmoke spurting up from four positions on an opposite ridge, and he motioned for the engineer to stop the train. He jumped down into cover and ran back to the flatcar, where possemen were leaping into cover.

'Over there, Billy!' Manning rasped. 'See the gunsmoke? Rally your men. Get the horses off the train and bring them across the gully. Send some of the posse to follow me!'

Drawing his sixgun, Manning ducked and ran from the side of the car, making to the left, and bullets struck the ground around him. He dived forward to roll into a depression, then slithered on his belly, crawling towards a gully. When he was out of sight of the four ambushers he got to his feet and ran swiftly, holding his gun ready. Sweat dripped down his fore-head as he glanced around, spotting some of the possemen already following him.

He pushed himself on with all haste while the shooting continued. Some of the possemen had dropped to cover around the train and were replying to the ambushers, and Manning was

149

satisfied that the attention of the badmen was being held.

When he paused it was only to check for drifting gunsmoke, and his teeth clicked together when he saw the ambushers had changed position. Slugs came whining at him, ricocheting off rocks, kicking up sand and dust, and he began to shoot, swinging his sixgun instinctively. He dropped to cover, marking the positions of the gunmen, and pushed forward, his mind completely free of fear. He thought coolly, intent only upon taking these troublemakers, for this was his job.

He saw a big figure rear up from behind a dun-coloured rock and turn to run. Clenching his teeth, he sent two slugs at the man, recognising Trig Forbes. His eyes glinted as he dropped under the menace of a hail of bullets from at least two other guns, but kept going forward, determined to get into close quarters. If he nailed Forbes now most of his troubles would be over. The thought was there in the forefront of his mind, and he was prepared to risk his life to bring about a speedy end to the situation. But Forbes dropped into a cluster of rocks and began to return fire again. Manning hunted cover and lay panting, waiting for the lethal storm to abate. Around him the possemen came moving up, and he grinned tightly, believing that Forbes could not get away.

Breaking his gun, he punched out the empty shells and reloaded the smoking weapon. Burnt powder was strong in his nostrils and he narrowed his eyes as he peered around. The ambushers had left their horses somewhere close by and they would be making for them now the surprise of their attack had gone. He eased forward, risking slugs as he endeavoured to get into a position from which to pin down the attackers.

The sounds of gunfire were heavy in the late afternoon, and smoke was drifting away on the hot breeze. Echoes mingled with fresh shots, and noise grumbled all the way to the horizon. Manning pushed up from a tall rock and a bullet splintered against it a few scant inches to the right of his head. Chips of rock sprayed into his face and he dropped flat, blood dripping down his forehead and chin. He crawled, ignoring the near misses, determined to get to grips with Forbes, and then he almost blundered headfirst into a ravine. He halted and peered down, thrusting his gunhand forward to empty the big sixgun at the four riders streaking away into the distance.

None of his shots scored and, as he reloaded, the quartet

vanished around a bend in the ravine. Manning drew a long breath, finished reloading, then stood up. All about him men were getting to their feet, and by degrees the shooting died away.

Billy Dainton arrived, leading his horse and Manning's. The deputy was grim-faced, but excitement blazed in his narrowed eyes. Manning checked his girth and sprang into his saddle.

'Come on,' he commanded. 'They're getting away. Leave someone to guard the train and the prisoner, Billy.'

He did not pause to see if his orders were carried out but rode along the top of the ravine in the direction the four men had taken. As he moved he studied the bottom of the depression. Dust was streaming into the air, marking the progress of the fleeing ambushers, and Manning gritted his teeth as he figured that now he had Forbes within his grasp.

When he glanced back he saw five mounted possemen following, led by Billy Dainton, and he grinned and pushed on, following the great gash in the ground, twice spotting Forbes and his three companions below, and he saw that they were not drawing away.

Two miles on the ravine began to flatten out. Manning pushed his horse harder, wanting to draw within good rifle range by the time the floor of the ravine reached his level. He wiped sweat out of his eyes, and when he glanced at the back of his hand he saw blood mingled with the sweat. His face was stinging in places and he could feel the stiffness of dried blood, but he was not seriously hurt and his pulses raced as he urged on his horse.

He could easily recognise Trig Forbes as one of the riders, and spurred his horse to greater effort. The big outlaw was there for the taking! The other three would be those men who had accompanied Forbes on the bank raid in Gadson Flats when Hart Loman died in the street. Manning steeled himself, and when the four began to ascend to his level he drew his sixgun and prepared to fight it out.

But it was long shooting for a pistol and he holstered the gun and set himself to get more speed from his mount. Dust flew and drifted in the air as he continued, and the dust cloud left by the four fleeing riders marked their passage ahead.

They were angling away towards the hills, and Manning nodded grimly, glancing back over his shoulder to find the possemen stringing out to his rear. None of them was as well mounted as he, and although his horse was weary after many days of travelling, he was making up a little ground on the outlaws.

Forbes twisted in his saddle and peered back, and Manning grinned. There would be no escape for the big man this time. He drew his sixgun again, lifting it and firing at extreme range. The crash of the shot sounded powerful in the stillness, and gunsmoke puffed into his face. There was no visible effect of the shot and he held his fire, aware that he was wasting lead.

But Forbes had jerked his rifle from its saddleboot, and Manning awaited the big man's next move, urging on his horse and getting a response, seeming to draw closer to the fleeing quartet. But Manning could feel that his horse was almost done, and when Billy Dainton finally drew alongside, then began to go on, Manning realised that he had lost out. He tightened his lips, watching the four fugitives, waiting for a flat stretch of ground that would give him time to halt and use his rifle, but the terrain was rough and rocky, and he knew the men would disappear behind cover before he could get his long gun into action.

He kept on riding, intent upon killing the animal if its death would take him within range of Forbes. Dainton drew twenty yards ahead, and Manning kept up the pressure on his own mount. Perhaps the outlaws had also been pushing their horses too hard in the past few days! But something had to give. The fast, strength-sapping pace could not be maintained indefinitely.

A rifle cracked, and Manning jerked up his head and saw Billy Dainton falling out of his saddle. There was a puff of gunsmoke ahead, between the four fugitives and the deputy. Manning gritted his teeth as his mount leaped over Dainton's body, but he did not look down.

Holstering his pistol, Manning lifted his Winchester from its saddleboot, loading the weapon, and dropped his knotted reins across the neck of his horse, guiding it with his knees. He raised his rifle and sought Forbes's big, powerful body. Several times he reached the point of squeezing the trigger when the wavering foresight seemed to find its mark on Forbes's target area, but each time the outlaw changed direction or disappeared behind rocks. It was the same with the other three men, and Manning patiently awaited his chance, aware that he was driving his horse to the very limits of its endurance.

Then they hit a flat stretch of ground before a long ridge, and Manning fired at Forbes. He did not see the result of the shot, but Forbes immediately pulled his horse down to a canter, slowing, turning to bring his weapon to bear. Manning kneed his mount to the left, losing speed quickly and, as he pressed behind a cluster of tall rocks, he yanked on his reins to stop the horse and vacated the saddle in a reckless leap. He crashed against a rock and slid sideways, landing with breath-smashing force on the ground, but he rolled and twisted, pushing himself forward until he could see what was happening. The four riders had halted and were turning to take on the strung-out posse. Manning grinned, cuffing back his stetson. He was in cover and the outlaws were out in the open.

Forbes cut loose, sending a stream of lead across the space between them, splattering the rocks with crackling slugs. Manning could not be cowed by near misses and lifted his rifle, drawing a bead on the big outlaw. But Forbes was no greenhorn, and was already swinging his mount again. Manning fired as the outlaw wheeled away. Forbes used brute strength to lift the animal's forefeet off the ground, and Manning's bullet took the horse through the head as it reared to shield Forbes's chest. The animal went down heavily and Forbes stepped out of the saddle and disappeared like a mountain lion amongst the rocks.

Manning swung his rifle to cover the other three outlaws, dismissing Forbes for the moment. He cut loose, his lips thin against his teeth, his left eye closed, the long gun steady in his hands. He hit one of the three, saw the man sway then pitch sideways out of leather, and he swung his aim to another. But they were fast disappearing behind cover, and soon there was only drifting gunsmoke to mark their previous position.

Gritting his teeth, Manning began to move, wanting to get after Forbes. He carried his rifle in his left hand, reaching for his Colt with his right. Hooves were pounding hard ground as some of the possemen came up to join in, and Manning felt a wave of satisfaction, for it looked as if Forbes was on foot and trapped in the rocks.

Then something struck his head with the force of a mulekick.

He felt the impact and his sense of balance vanished. For an interminable moment he had no idea if he was on his head or his feet. Then a great black pit opened up at his side and he seemed to dive straight into it, to be encompassed by silent oblivion.

Chapter Fifteen

A shouting voice brought Manning to consciousness, and he opened his eyes, his mind strangely blank for several moments. He was dizzy and there was a pain in the left side of his head. As he gazed around he became aware that he was being held in an unbreakable grip. He was on his feet, sagging against someone built like a grizzly bear. There was a shimmering mist before his eyes, blurring his sight, and a groan escaped him as he shook his head, an action which sent a blinding shaft of pain searing through his skull.

The voice was still shouting, and by degrees Manning found the words making sense. A thrill of horror cut through the layers of shock in his mind as he recognised Trig Forbes's harsh tones, and his sight cleared as he began to take in the reality of the situation. Lifting his head, he saw that Forbes was holding him with a powerful arm around his chest, and a nagging pain in Manning's side was caused by the muzzle of a pistol which Forbes was holding jammed against him.

'That's better!' Forbes was yelling. 'If anyone makes a wrong move then Manning gets it. Back off from those horses! Make it fast or I'll do some killing.'

Manning slitted his eyes, his forehead wrinkled in a frown against the pain in his skull. He looked around and saw some of the possemen peering from cover, guns held helplessly in their hands, and as he straightened the gun dug even harder into his side.

'Okay, Manning, I got you dead to rights!' Forbes rasped in his ear. 'If you don't want to die here and now you better do like I tell you. We're getting on a couple of broncs and riding out of here. I saw Glory Harpe being held on that train back there and I want her. You and me are gonna get her.'

Manning drew a swift breath. He peered around, still dizzy, then called at the possemen.

'Shoot him down!' he shouted. 'Don't let him get away.'

'He'll kill you, Chet!' one of the men retorted. 'We can't do it.'

'Where's Billy Dainton?' Manning gritted his teeth as he looked for the deputy.

'He's dead,' someone replied. 'I checked him. He was shot out of his saddle.'

'I killed him!' Forbes announced. 'And I'll do some more killing if I have to. Now let's get moving, Manning. These punks won't lift a finger to do anything against me. We're getting out of here.'

Manning felt the strength in Forbes's left hand as it tightened around his chest, and he could scarcely breathe. The menace of the gun in his back warned him that it would be fatal to disobey, and now his mind was clearing he began to think straight once more. He drew a painful breath.

'Okay, you men!' he called. 'Don't get yourselves shot up on my account. Let Forbes go!'

'That's better!' Forbes relaxed his grip slightly. 'One of you possemen check out Snap Dillon for me. I saw him go out of his saddle.'

Someone moved away through the rocks as Forbes forced Manning towards the spot where several saddle horses were standing with trailing reins. A few moments later a hard voice reported that Dillon was dead.

'Okay, now we're pulling out,' Forbes said. 'You possemen get away from here before I start shooting. If anyone tries to stop me then Manning gets it.'

Manning tightened his lips, not wanting to resist now. He was hoping his chance would come before Forbes got clear. They reached the horses and the possemen were still crouching in cover, watching intently. But Forbes did not swing up into the saddle. He kept a horse between himself and the possemen, motioning for Manning to lead two of the animals, and they started away amongst the rocks. A gun crashed before they had moved many yards, and Manning looked around swiftly, to find that Forbes had shot down the fourth horse to prevent pursuit. The big outlaw was grinning as he finally swung into the saddle.

'Okay, Manning!' he grated, his heavy, stubbled face twisted with passion, 'Climb on and lead that other hoss. It's for

156

Glory. Me and you are going back to the train to pick her up.'

Manning mounted and led the third horse, riding ahead of Forbes, who held his gun ready. They started back towards the track, and when they were clear of the area where the possemen had been, Forbes relaxed a little and came closer to Manning.

'The big hero!' he jeered. 'Bossman of the railroad! Well you ain't so tough! I knocked you over with a rock! So you and your boys was gonna take care of me and my new gang, huh?' He chuckled harshly. 'You got no hope, Manning! When I bust Glory free from that posse at the train I'm handing you over to her. I'm gonna get a lot of fun out of watching you die. She ain't gonna be in no hurry over it, neither. I figure you'll last mebbe an hour before she finishes you off. Then when you're out of the way we can take over the railroad!'

'You'll never do that,' Manning retorted, glancing around. 'Kill me and you've still got some more men equally as good as me to buck. You ain't as good a leader as Yaro, and look what happened to him.'

'You did me a good turn there!' Forbes chuckled, evidently well pleased with the way his fortunes had turned. 'I allus figured myself to be a better man than Yaro, and you got rid of him for me! He wasn't so smart! He had Willard Blaine getting information for him, and I got me someone who will do the same when you're out of the way.'

'Someone working for the railroad?' Manning winced as he turned his head quickly to stare at the big outlaw.

'Never mind!' Forbes growled.

'He would have to be a railroad employee,' Manning countered, 'or he wouldn't be able to get the information. Who have you made a deal with?'

'Now you're asking!' Forbes grinned crookedly, his eyes blazing with elation.

Manning lifted a hand to his head. His probing fingers discovered a large bump above his left temple where the rock Forbes hurled at him had made contact, and blood had dried on his face. His head ached now, and he was compelled to narrow his eyes against the sunlight. For some time they rode in silence, until they topped a rise and saw before them the train waiting on the track.

'Hold it right there!' Forbes ordered. He came up beside

Manning, peering down at the scene before them, his gun still covering Manning although his attention was momentarily diverted.

Manning eased his feet out of his stirrups, prepared to take any chance that came his way. He steeled himself for the effort it would take to get at Forbes as the big outlaw spoke harshly.

'There ain't no one but a posseman and the engineer and fireman down there, apart from the men we hit when we started the ambush,' Forbes mused. 'I can handle them, Manning! So much for your troubleshooting, huh? We've played up hell today. Pulled down some telegraph poles and shot up two trains. We must have killed a dozen railroad men!'

Manning froze at the grim news, and Forbes glanced at him, grinning tightly, his eyes wide with vicious pleasure. The big outlaw waggled his gun.

'That's right! Makes you look poor, huh? That's what we want. There's a man ready to step into your boots who'll do a lot for us after we've proved you ain't no great shakes at troubleshooting!'

Manning took a swift breath as Forbes glanced down at the scene below again, and eased his left boot out of its stirrup, kicking sideways and upwards with his dusty toe, aiming for the pistol in Forbes's hand. The gunhand was just within range, and Manning's boot made contact with Forbes's wrist. The big man cursed as his sixgun flew out of his hand and he started around to face Manning, his reaction instinctive. But Manning was already moving, snatching on his reins, pulling his mount around and causing it to rear. The animal was startled by the unexpected rough treatment and cannoned against Forbes's horse, sending it to its knees on the edge of the slope. Forbes yelled wildly as he felt his balance going, but his left hand snatched out his second pistol.

Gritting his teeth, Manning left his saddle in a desperate leap, his hands outstretched to grapple with the big man. He caught Forbes around the neck, his fast-moving weight completing the tumble Forbes was taking. The outlaw kicked his feet clear of his stirrups as the horse lunged sideways, and he hit the ground under Manning.

Aware of the gun in the big man's left hand, Manning reared up, reaching for the gun arm with his right hand. At the same time he sledged his left fist against Forbes's stubbled chin. The

158

blow had little effect and Forbes bawled with rage as he arched his back and flung Manning clear. Manning retained a grip on Forbes's gun arm, forcing the weapon away from his body. Forbes came over, rolling to gain the advantage, and Manning twisted sideways as the bigger man tried to land astride him.

Forbes was growling like an animal and he dragged his left hand free of Manning's grip, swinging the big pistol to batter it against Manning's skull. Wriggling sideways, Manning was aware that he had no chance against this tough man pound for pound, and he was not going to be lured into a test of strength. He was panting as he got up to one knee, still clinging to Forbes's left wrist, and before the bigger man could make another move he straightened and kicked viciously, catching Forbes's face. The outlaw roared and thrust hard, getting up from the dusty ground. Manning kneed him in the chest, still trying to snatch the pistol from the powerful grip, and Forbes went down again, yelling in fury.

Manning pushed the man's gunhand to the ground and stamped upon it, driving his heel against it, trying to break the powerful grip upon the weapon, and Forbes twisted with his shoulders on the ground and kicked up at Manning's face with both feet. Manning anticipated the move and ducked under the feet, twisting Forbes's gunhand around under the man's back, and when the outlaw's legs came down the gun arm was pinioned between his heavy body and the ground.

Pushing to his knees, Manning exerted pressure on the arm, causing Forbes to groan, and suddenly the big man was ceasing his struggles, trying to twist around to relieve the pressure on his left arm. Manning leaned over him, attempting to pin him down with his weight, and Forbes reached up with his right hand to gouge at Manning's eyes. For a few tense moments they strained one against the other, panting, groaning, cursing and writhing. Manning's sight was blurring again, and sweat ran down his face. He knew he was in no condition for a prolonged battle with this massively built man, and eased up suddenly, grasping Forbes by the shirt front and swinging up his knee, slamming it into the man's face. Four times in quick succession he caught the outlaw, and felt Forbes's nose give with the second blow. There was a sharp pain in his knee cap at the impact, but he kept attacking, knowing he had to win this quickly or lose every chance of success.

Forbes managed to squirm off his back, and his left arm came from beneath his body, still gripping the pistol. But the limb had been weakened and Manning forced it aside. He was breathing through his mouth now. His arms felt heavy and powerless. He twisted Forbes's left arm, levering against the elbow joint, and the gun finally fell from the big hand and thudded into the dust.

Kicking the pistol aside, Manning threw himself after it, getting his right hand to it, but Forbes was like a big cat and came hurtling at him, hands outstretched, face contorted with the effort. Manning dropped on to his back, still grabbing the gun, and raised his legs as Forbes reached him, thrusting his feet into the bigger man's stomach and sending him in a high arc over his head. He twisted around, lifting the gun, covering Forbes and, despite his weariness, a tight grin tugged at his mouth.

'Got you!' he rasped, levelling the gun, and the outlaw paused in the rush to his feet, halting and clenching his hands, for there was a space of several feet between them and the black muzzle of the big sixgun was now lined up steadily at his chest. 'That's right,' Manning continued, pushing himself to one knee. 'Get your hands up high and keep 'em there! Looks to me like you've come to the end of your rope, big man!'

'Don't count on it,' a harsh voice rasped from behind Manning, and he turned his head quickly, freezing when he saw two men sitting their mounts some yards away, both holding levelled guns. 'Never figured I'd see the day a man could beat Trig Forbes, but you got him took, Manning. Too bad for you we stuck around. But Trig has got quite a future planned for us.' Hemp Arrel hardened his tone. 'Just drop that gun or we'll drop you!'

Manning took a deep breath, then opened his right hand and let the pistol fall to the ground. He got to his feet as Forbes came forward, grinning now, although his face was covered with blood and his nose had swollen and looked crooked. There was a cold sensation in Manning's belly as Forbes scooped up the big gun and cocked it, jamming the muzzle into Manning's side.

'I've got a mind to blow you apart!' he snarled. 'If it wasn't for the pleasure I'll get watching Glory cut you to pieces you'd be dead right now. But I can wait. We're going down to the

160

train to grab Glory then we'll make tracks, and this will be your last day on earth!' He grinned at the two riders as Manning moved to the horses. 'Figured you'd run out on me, Hemp!' he commented.

'Not us!' Arrel retorted. 'Where's Snap?'

'Dead. He stopped a slug in that shoot-out where we turned. I guess that's the way it goes, huh?'

Arrel and Santor exchanged glances, and they came forward as Manning and Forbes mounted up.

'We didn't count on all this trouble, Trig,' Arrel said thinly. 'There's gonna be hell to pay for what's happened around here. I figure with Dillon gone we better move out pronto, huh?'

'We got a deal!' Forbes spoke harshly, wiping blood from his face. His pistol covered Manning, who sat his mount wearily, his shoulders slumped. 'I tell you it will pan out the way I got it roped. That man back in Jules Crossing. With Manning dead he'll step into the big saddle with the railroad. Then there'll be no holding us!'

'Well let's get away from here now,' Arrel suggested. 'I got a feeling there will be more trouble coming along that track before too long.'

'Let's go pick up the woman,' Forbes said, motioning with his gun for Manning to precede him.

Manning rode down the slope towards the train. He could see Glory sitting on the flatcar. The engineer and the fireman were standing on the footplate, watching the track, and the posseman left to guard Glory was standing by the flatcar, a rifle in his hands. A couple of men, slightly wounded, were sitting on one end of the flatcar, both holding pistols.

As they drew nearer, Hemp Arrel lifted his rifle and shot the posseman guarding Glory. At the crash of the shot the two possemen on the car lifted their pistols, and Manning flinched as Forbes cut loose at them, his first shot downing one, his third nailing the other. The two railroad men on the footplate raised their hands, and Manning was grim-faced as they rode in.

'Just stay quiet and you won't get hurt!' Forbes yelled at the railroaders. 'Glory, are you hurt?'

The girl was sitting up, staring at Manning, and he could see hatred in her pale features. She got to her feet and jumped down from the car, moving to the horse Manning was leading, and, as she swung into the saddle, her eyes glittered balefully.

Manning studied her impassively, knowing that his life was at stake now, but he showed no feelings and Forbes chuckled as they wheeled away.

'Ride beside Manning!' he called. 'Keep going until we're out of range of the train, Glory. Ben, you stay at their backs and keep Manning covered.'

Manning glanced around as he continued, and the woman at his side was hard-faced, stiff in her saddle. Ben Santor followed some yards behind, a gun in his hand, his face bleak and alert. Forbes and Hemp Arrel were together beside the train, covering the men there and watching their surroundings. A sigh escaped Manning and he straightened his aching body. He felt as if he had been knocked down by a runaway train. There was a throbbing in his head, a throbbing agony in the bruises he had collected. But his mind was a ferment of frustration. He had come so close to nailing Trig Forbes. Now he was in trouble and his future was grim. He tried not to think of what must lay before him and watched for a chance to escape. He might get one opportunity before they killed him, and no matter how slim it might be he would have to take it.

'Looks like you're getting your wish granted, Glory!' he said in a low voice, and the woman glanced at him, her expression taut, her eyes narrowed and filled with a hard glitter.

'You figure I won't go through with it?' She smiled mirthlessly. 'Don't kid yourself. Ben is in his grave because of you! I'll kill you by inches! You'll wish you'd never been born before I get done with you.'

He smiled tightly, glancing back towards the train. Forbes was still beside the engine, the other outlaw at his side, and now a hundred yards separated them. Letting his gaze move slightly, he took in the stocky figure of Ben Santor just behind, holding a sixgun in his right hand, and his pale eyes narrowed as he calculated his chances. He wouldn't get a better opportunity than this. When Forbes and the other hardcase arrived the odds against him would be trebled.

But he could not tackle the outlaw from this distance. Manning desperately weighed his chances. He was not afraid to die doing his job, but he needed a percentage for survival in his favour. He glanced at Glory again, turning cold as he saw her expression. Her face was utterly merciless.

'Think about it,' she said crisply. 'Just think of what I'm

gonna do to you, Manning. I want you to know fear and agony before you go. I'll make it slow and hard. It'll be tough on you! And Trig will sit around watching. He's that type.'

'I know his type and you don't,' Manning warned. 'You're gonna be mighty sorry you threw in with him when he starts getting ideas about you. You met Hank Bolden while you were in Jules Crossing jail, huh? Well Bolden knew Forbes back in Texas, and he told me just what kind of a man Trig is. He can't help himself when there is a woman around. He'll show you his true colour before he gets through.'

'But you won't be around to say I told you so!' she retorted.

Manning sighed and shook his head. He was getting nowhere fast. He glanced at the stocky outlaw again, wary of the man's alert manner, knowing that he would not be able to get to grips before the sixgun in his hand exploded in a death roar. He glanced back towards the train, feeling a sense of urgency beginning to take hold of him. Forbes was still there with the third outlaw, but it would not be long now before he left the scene and caught up. Then it would be too late!

At that moment a gun crashed behind them by the train, and Manning saw a figure fall limply from the footplate. The stocky outlaw behind him swung in his saddle to see what was happening and, before he was aware of his actions, Manning had wheeled his mount and spurred it towards his captor. He ducked as the man sensed the movement and returned his attention to his own business, the heavy Colt lifting menacingly. It exploded as Manning's horse crashed against the outlaw's mount, and the bullet tugged at Manning's dusty stetson.

The impact between the two horses was so great that the outlaw's animal was flung to the ground, taking its stocky rider with it. Manning leaped out of the saddle, filled with desperation. He saw the outlaw's horse roll over, pinning its rider to the hard ground for a moment, but the sixgun in the man's hand was pointing in Manning's direction.

Gritting his teeth, Manning hurled himself forward as the horse began to arise, and he landed on the outlaw's gun arm with both feet. The man yelled with pain, his pistol forgotten, and Manning fell and rolled in the dust, grabbing desperately at the gun. His fingers touched it and he scrabbled for it, losing it as his momentum carried him on. He stopped and squirmed around, to find the outlaw springing up, cursing loudly and dragging a knife from a sheath at his belt.

Manning got to his knees and lunged for the pistol again, getting it this time, lifting it and cocking it with one experienced movement. Sunlight glinted on the blade of the knife as the outlaw came for him, and Manning dropped back to avoid the first vicious lunge, feeling the wind of the near-miss as he moved. He landed on his back, the gun steady in his right hand, and as the outlaw regained his balance and came at him again, Manning shot him in the chest. The man went sprawling, the point of the knife sticking into the ground a scant foot from Manning's side.

Breathing heavily, Manning pushed himself on to one knee, looking around swiftly. Glory was sitting her mount, hands clenched, eyes narrowed as she awaited the outcome of the struggle. Manning peered around. The echoes of a second shot were drifting away from the train. He clenched his teeth, aware that Forbes was shooting all survivors back there. He lunged to his feet and ran to the stocky outlaw's horse, stepping over the motionless body of the dead man to snatch at the rifle snug in the man's saddleboot.

A chance had come, he knew, and it would not improve. He had a couple of guns and Trig Forbes was within range. It was all he could ask for. But he forgot about Glory Harpe as he grabbed the rifle and turned to use it.

Chapter Sixteen

Forbes and Hemp Arrel were riding towards Manning now, and Forbes was in a sweat of excitement. He had cold-bloodedly shot the rest of the men around the train. But Arrel was anxious, having seen the fight between Manning and Ben Santor, and when Manning ran to Santor's horse and dragged the rifle from the saddleboot the outlaw called to Forbes.

'Manning is loose again! He's got a rifle, Trig!'

'Ride him down!' Forbes rasped, spurring his mount and ducking low in the saddle. 'We got to nail him, Hemp.'

Manning jacked a brass-bound cartridge into the chamber of the rifle as the two outlaws came galloping towards him. Both were low in their saddles, and Forbes was already triggering his sixgun, sending a string of shots that chased out the silence. Gunsmoke drifted. Manning dropped to his knees. Spurts of dust marked where the shots were striking, and some were very close to him. His eyes were narrowed, his lips pulled tight as he lifted the rifle to his shoulder.

He was cool inside despite the sense of urgency which gripped him. Firing, he swung his rifle to allow for the movement of the riders, and his first bullet took Forbes's horse in the chest. The animal went down, slithering along the hard ground, tossing Forbes clear, and Manning did not watch for results but swung his rifle, intent upon nailing Arrel. The second outlaw was shooting now, his sixgun belching fire. A bullet struck Manning's empty holster, the impact jerking him out of his aim, and he dropped flat as he recovered, his attention on the speeding rider. The distance between them was lessening rapidly, but Manning was calm. He peered through his back-sight and aligned the foresight on Hemp Arrel's chest, his line of aim between the ears of the rapidly approaching horse. Arrel was shooting and yelling wildly in an attempt to throw Manning off.

Manning fired. He opened his left eye to check the shot and saw Arrel rearing up in his saddle, gun spilling from his hand, arms flying wide. The outlaw's hat fell from his head as he pitched sideways. His left foot kicked free of the stirrup as he went down but the right foot caught, and the next instant the horse was galloping away to the nearest ridge, raising dust as it dragged the lifeless body.

Relief began to seep into Manning's mind. He reloaded, returning his attention to Forbes, taking a swift, smoke-laden breath when he spotted the big outlaw on his feet once more, coming forward at a crouching run with a sixgun ready in his hand. But in the back of his mind a nagging thought distracted him from the matter in hand and he wondered at it even as he covered Forbes. Something was wrong: his fighting instincts were trying to warn him, but he had to nail Forbes. He lifted the rifle as the big man began to shoot once more and, as he concentrated upon drawing a bead upon the man, something crashed against the back of his head.

The rifle spilled from his hands. He had a vague impression of a figure at his side and turned his head as he pitched forward on to his face in the dust. He caught a glimpse of Glory standing there, a chunk of rock in her hands, her face white and taut with desperation, and he knew a pang of despair as darkness exploded inside his skull and he lost consciousness.

When he came to he was in a crazy world of dizziness, pain, and jolting motion. His head throbbed agonisingly and he felt sick. Opening his eyes, Manning discovered that he could see little, but he could hear the familiar sound of a train hammering along the track. He blinked, his alertness returning, and he discovered that his hands were bound behind his back.

He was lying in a boxcar that was filled practically to overflowing with supplies. There was just a narrow corridor of space down one side, from the door to the ladder leading up to the small hatch in the roof. The sun was going down, he figured, judging by the lack of light, then he became aware of someone just beyond his range of vision. He stifled a groan as he moved slightly to see Glory sitting on a crate by his head.

'So you're awake!' she snapped. 'I was wondering when you were gonna come out of it. I thought I'd hit you too hard and you was dying. But you ain't gonna cheat me out of my pleasure.'

'What's happening?' he demanded. 'How is it we're on a train? Where are we heading? Who's driving the locomotive?'

'Now you're asking, and I'm gonna tell you because I want you to know just how badly you've failed. Call yourself a troubleshooter! You couldn't have done worse if you'd tried.'

'For God's sake cut out the gloating!' he rasped. 'Just tell me what's going on.'

'The train the posse was on went off the track at the first bend. Trig drove it fast and derailed it. Then we waited for the next supply train to come along and, when it stopped at the derailment, Trig killed the railroaders on it. And guess what? We looked in this boxcar and found it's stacked from floor to roof with blasting powder. So Trig got the idea of running it smack into the construction camp at the end of the track. It'll go off the rails and explode, and there won't be a lot of your camp left, huh? We're still working for Western Pacific, Manning. Just because Ben is dead doesn't mean the contract ran out. I'm gonna collect in Ben's place, and I'm gonna start peeling the hide off you in little strips now you've come back to your senses.'

The hatch in the roof was suddenly dragged aside, permitting a shaft of dim light to enter the boxcar, and Manning suppressed a groan as he looked around. There were kegs of blasting powder and boxes of dynamite stacked inside the car. He watched Trig Forbes descending the ladder, and the big outlaw grinned when he saw that Manning was conscious.

'I got the train running smoothly,' he said. 'I'm gonna set fuses amongst this lot and light them when we're ready to jump the train as it runs into the end of the track.' He turned and busied himself, and Manning, watching intently, soon realised that Forbes knew a great deal about explosives. The outlaw tied several sticks of dynamite together and put a cap and fuse on the centre stick. He made three such bundles and planted them amongst the stacked kegs.

'I wouldn't want to be within a mile of this lot when it goes up,' Forbes said when he had completed his preparations. 'Can you imagine what it'll do to your camp at end of track, Manning? It'll make a worse mess than that herd of cattle we drove through the other camp.' He chuckled harshly. 'If you're gonna kill him, Glory, then you better get on with it, because he's staying on the train when we get off. I figure we'll be running into end of track in an hour.'

Glory drew a knife from a sheath on her belt and smiled as she faced Manning, who struggled with the rope around his wrists. But, as the woman took a step towards him, Forbes grasped her wrist.

'It ain't gonna take you long to do for him,' he rasped. 'I figure I'm entitled to a little of your time before we get to end of track. Let's get down on that crate over there.'

'Are you crazy?' she demanded, trying to thrust him away.

'I've done everything you wanted. You've got Manning, and we're gonna put a stop to the S & W again. So I want something, and now.'

Forbes encircled her with his arms as he spoke, and Glory cursed him, struggling to break free. Manning watched hopefully, ready to take advantage of any opportunity which might come his way. Then Glory slashed at Forbes with the knife, drawing blood from his left shoulder and narrowly missing his left ear. He jerked his head aside just in time, and uttered an oath as he struck her across the face with the back of one massive hand. The girl fell instantly and Forbes bent over her, ripping at her clothes.

'You'll do what I want,' he snarled, and turned a leering gaze upon Manning. 'I've heard that you're quite a man with the women, huh? Well this time you can watch.'

He ripped the pants off Glory, who was groaning as she slowly regained her senses. Manning gazed at the woman's nude body, remembering the time he had made love to her, but all his thoughts were turned towards escaping. If he could get free of his bonds he would finish this.

Forbes picked up the naked woman as if she were a child and thrust her face down across a crate, then opened up his Levi's. He turned his head to grin at Manning as he spread Glory's legs. There was an eager expression upon his face. He grasped Glory's hips from behind, lifting her bodily to his level, her face pressing against the crate. He pulled her backwards towards him. When he failed to penetrate he chuckled and raised her higher, then worked his hips, thrusting at her with all his strength.

Passion caught him then and he sweated and groaned as he worked at her. She tried to get away from him but his powerful hands held her motionless. Her face was contorted with pain and fury. Manning, watching intently, could not fail to be moved by the sight, and clenched his teeth at the faint stirrings of lust within his own loins. But he renewed his attack upon the rope binding his wrists, aware that his last moments were upon him if he could not break free.

Forbes relieved himself with no more than a dozen vicious thrusts then threw Glory sideways. The woman fell across Manning's legs, her flesh glistening with sweat. Forbes grinned, picking up her discarded shirt to wipe himself. Then he flung the shirt into her face.

'If you ain't careful, Glory, you'll stay aboard this train with Manning when it goes up. You better get it into your head that when I want you I ain't gonna take no for an answer.'

He turned to check the fuses he had set, and Glory pushed herself to her hands and knees, reaching for the knife she had dropped when Forbes hit her. She found it and started to her feet, moving with the litheness of a big cat, and Manning clenched his teeth as she struck at Forbes's back with the glinting blade. It was more a slash than a stab, and caught Forbes high in the left shoulder, where bloodstains were already beginning to congeal.

Forbes cursed and swung around, crashing his fist against Glory's chin, and when she fell to the floor like a rag doll, the knife spinning from her grasp, he bent and took her by the neck, biting his bottom lip as fury exploded in his mind. His massive hands tightened inexorably around Glory's throat, his thumbs digging into her soft flesh, and Manning moved his left leg slightly to conceal the discarded knife, which lay within his reach.

Forbes was growling in his throat, his control gone, and he shook Glory several times without releasing the pressure he was applying to her neck.

'You'll kill her,' Manning warned, but Forbes was deaf to his words.

When the spate of rage passed, Forbes dropped the woman to the floor. He stared down at her for a moment, breathing heavily, blinking his eyes. Then he bent over her and felt for a heartbeat. He looked up at Manning, his face contorted with passion.

'She's dead,' he announced. 'It was her damn fault. She

169

went too far. She wasn't gonna get away with treating me like trash. It was all right for you to have her, and Ben let me have her to keep me sweet. But she wouldn't let me have her for my own sake.'

He turned to the door and slid it open, then kicked the lifeless body out of the car. Manning watched, his face set in harsh lines, and Forbes faced him once more.

'I wanta see you dead, Manning,' he muttered. 'But it don't matter to me how you go so long as you do. I'm leaving you in here with the explosives. You'll go with a bang.'

Manning remained silent and Forbes turned to the ladder leading up to the hatch in the roof. He climbed it, pausing for a moment at the top to look around in the last of the day's light.

'Say, they really got a move on with this track, huh?' He glanced down at Manning. 'I can see the Chamos Mountains dead ahead, and the track runs straight down here. It's a long downgrade and the construction camp is at the end of it. I'll be back shortly to light the fuses. I got to time this real good to get the explosion after the train hits the camp.'

He climbed out through the hatch and went forward to the locomotive. Manning at once reached for the knife, but found it almost impossible to grasp with his hands tied behind his back. Twice he dropped it and had to fumble for it, and when he did manage to get it firmly held he dug the point of it into his left wrist instead of bringing the keen edge of the blade across the rope. But he persevered, and fancied that he was making some progress. He knew by the level of the floor that the train was travelling faster and faster along a downgrade, and in his mind's eye he picked out their exact position. This downgrade was about four miles long. He remembered seeing it when he visited a surveyor's camp a couple of months earlier. So Ike Mozee had managed to push this far! He could understand why Western Pacific were perturbed by the S & W's progress.

Forbes's feet and legs suddenly appeared in the hatch, and Manning dropped the knife and lay upon it. He leaned back his head and closed his eyes, remaining motionless until he heard Forbes's harsh chuckle. Then he stirred. The big outlaw was standing before him, grinning.

'So you've accepted it, huh?' Forbes demanded. 'I guess there ain't much you can do. So this is the way it's gonna end,

Manning. All the good men who have tried to nail you! I don't know why they found it so hard. I'm gonna kill you off. You won't be around to see it, but this whole territory will be under my thumb after I've finished this. We're hammering down the grade now, and nothing can stop this train. Those fuses will burn long enough, if my timing is right. See you in Hell, huh?'

He turned to light the fuses, and when they were spluttering he went back to the ladder, half-turning to grin at Manning.

'I'm gonna open up the throttle real wide now and jump,' he said. 'So long, sucker!'

Manning strained at the rope as Forbes ascended the ladder, then reached for the knife again. It took him several seconds to work it back into position, and he sawed against the rope, wishing he could put some strength behind his actions. The fuses were burning and time was running out fast. Even if he managed to get free and extinguish the fuses the crash at the end of track would smash the boxcar to splinters, and one spark was all that would be needed to detonate this deadly load.

The rope gave slightly and he dropped the knife, using his strength, gritting his teeth, his muscles standing out under the strain. A pulse throbbed in his temple and he closed his eyes, feeling sweat splashing from his brow. Then the rope parted and his wrists flew apart. He stumbled to his feet, cursing when he discovered that his circulation had been restricted by the rope. His hands were practically numb.

He staggered to where the fuses were burning and jerked them free, hurling them out of the open doorway. He could see the last glow of the sun in the western sky as he turned and picked up the knife. He had to stop the train, and if Forbes was still on the locomotive then he meant to take the badman as well.

Climbing the ladder, he stuck his head through the hatch and peered around, satisfying himself that he had guessed correctly the position of the train. They were hammering down that long downgrade, and at the bottom lay the unsuspecting construction camp.

Manning slid through the hatch, keeping low. He sprang on to the tender, gritting his teeth when he saw Forbes still at the controls of the engine. The outlaw was peering ahead, his hand upon the throttle, and Manning flexed his fingers and sprang forward, yelling as he closed with Forbes.

171

The outlaw swung around quickly, reaching for the sixgun in his holster. He blocked Manning's thrust with the knife and the cold steel flipped away and went spinning to the ground beside the track. The next instant Forbes was bringing his .45 into play and Manning grasped the bigger man's wrist and forced the muzzle aside. The weapon exploded as Forbes squeezed the trigger but the bullet flew wide, striking a metal part of the engine and screeching away in protest. Forbes was cursing. They were in half-light, with a faint glow coming from the firebox. The train sped along the track, gaining speed all the time, jolting and leaping on the rails as gravity aided the engine. They were going down steeply, and Manning fought with the strength of desperation, aware that if he managed to beat Forbes he still had to prevent the train running out of track.

Forbes was trying to bring the muzzle of his gun towards Manning, who twisted sideways and used both hands to grasp Forbes's wrist. He bent the gun inwards, thrusting the muzzle against the outlaw's chest, and tried to slide a finger over Forbes's trigger finger. Forbes brought up his left knee, catching Manning in the groin, but the action broke the outlaw's stance and he lost balance, falling backwards against a stanchion. Manning jerked the sixgun around and thrust his right forefinger against the trigger. The weapon exploded with a heavy report and Forbes staggered as if a mule had kicked him.

Manning realised that the bullet had hit the outlaw, but the muzzle had been canted slightly upwards. Forbes swung away and the gun went flying from the cab. The next instant Forbes had secured a grip around Manning's neck, and his powerful fingers squeezed until coloured lights flashed before Manning's eyes.

Forbes used his greater height and weight to get Manning off balance and pressed back against the side of the cab. Manning tried to break the grip but soon realised that he was wasting time. Forbes had taken a hold no human could break. With his air cut off, Manning began to fall to his knees, and he knew that if he went down he was as good as finished.

His hands clawed at Forbes's wrists, then fell away to the man's body. He felt the stickiness of blood and fought against encroaching darkness that seemed filled with flashing lights. He was choking as Glory had done, and his reactions became

172

sluggish. But in the back of his mind a ray of light pinpointed a last desperate chance. He gripped Forbes's sticky shirt and sent his right forefinger in search of the bullet hole. There was a ragged tear in the shirt, and Manning thrust a finger into it, feeling the tip entering the wound. A broken rib was jagged and sharp, but Manning fought against the encompassing darkness of unconsciousness which was stealing in upon him and rammed his finger deeper into the wound.

Forbes gasped and moved his hands, enabling Manning to draw a quick breath which fed more oxygen to his starved brain. Drawing upon all his reserves of strength and determination, Manning jerked his finger and twisted it, driving it deeper into the bullet wound. He was almost upon his knees now, and Forbes was leaning over him, locking his elbows in a death grip and his fingers in a murderous hold.

Clenching his teeth, Manning tensed his right arm for a last effort. His lungs were palpitating, his head seeming to swell as veins became gorged with blood caused by the constriction around his neck. He used his trembling legs to thrust himself upright, bringing power to his arm, and then he lunged with his right arm, his forefinger stiffened. He felt something give inside Forbes's wound, and then his finger plunged into a pulpy mass. The broken rib jammed against the finger and Manning sweated as sight and sound began to fade. He knew he was going down again, and concentrated upon his finger. The next instant Forbes was releasing his grip and falling slackly upon Manning, who went down on the footplate and lay gasping for air.

When he pulled his finger from the hole in Forbes's chest, Manning knew it was broken, but he staggered to his feet, mouth agape, senses whirling. He fell against the controls, hitting the brakes hard and throwing the wheels into reverse. There was a screeching sound as the big drivers tried to spin, but they locked and the train skidded along the rails, throwing up showers of sparks. Metal scraped against metal, and Manning peered through the window, gulping when he saw how close they were to end of track. They were rapidly running out of rails. He hit the whistle cord, sounding short, urgent blasts, hoping to alert the camp to the danger that was speeding towards it.

The next instant the locomotive was passing Ike Mozee's

173

coach on the loop-line, and Manning hoped that the construction crews had laid a good day's quota of track. He saw figures appearing in the twilight but peered ahead, looking for the last of the rails. The train was decelerating, and Manning let go of the whistle cord and slumped against a stanchion. He looked down at the unconscious Trig Forbes and waited to see if the outlaw had won, for there was nothing else he could do. If he ran out of track there would be a pile-up, and that boxcar would blow the camp sky-high.

But the train stopped. Silence came, and Manning dared not look from the cab. They were still on the rails! The thought spun around in his mind and he drew a deep breath into his still aching lungs. His neck was sore, and he guessed he would wear bruises on it for many days to come. But there were voices yelling all around, and one he recognised was that of Asa Blaine.

'What in hell are you playing at, coming into camp at that speed?' Blaine demanded, climbing to the footplate, a gun in his hand, and he was followed closely by Ike Mozee. He halted when he recognised Manning. 'By God! Where did you come from?' He looked down at Forbes stretched out groaning on the floor.

'I've just finished that little chore you wanted me to handle,' Manning said in a hoarse voice, fingering his neck. 'There's Forbes, and Glory Harpe went off the train dead a few miles back. Trimble is also dead.'

'It's about time you cleared that up. What took you so long?' Blaine came forward and thrust a pugnacious jaw at Manning. 'Don't you know it's neck and neck between us and Western Pacific? And there are Indians around Apache Pass who probably won't want the railroad to go through there. You've got a hell of a lot to do, Chet, if Ike here is to make his deadlines. We're pushing on fast as we can, and it's a lucky thing for you we had a good day today. There's only about twenty feet of track in front of you. What were you trying to do, wreck this train and the whole camp? Don't you know that first boxcar is filled with explosives?'

'I had an idea it was,' Manning retorted, feeling relief beginning to ripple through him. He had done his job! Another threat to the smooth working of the S & W had been averted, but there were a few loose ends to be tidied. He needed to find out who on the railroad had been prepared to work with Forbes, and there were two young women in Buffalo Junction who would be waiting anxiously for news of him. He heaved a long sigh and turned to examine Forbes, who was unconscious and breathing heavily, blood high on his shirt front. 'Put him under tight guard,' he ordered. 'He sure is hard to kill, and I'll need to talk to him when he comes to. But he won't get out of jail again. This time there's no one left alive to help him.'

He heaved a long sigh and turned to climb down from the footplate. It came to him, as his feet touched the hard ground, that he had a future to look forward to once again, and he meant to live it up for all he was worth because there was no telling, in his business, when it would suddenly come to an end.

Wyndham Books are obtainable from many booksellers and newsagents. If you have any difficulty please send purchase price plus postage on the scale below to:

Wyndham Cash Sales,
P.O. Box 11,
Falmouth,
Cornwall

OR

Star Book Service,
G.P.O. Box 29,
Douglas,
Isle of Man,
British Isles

While every effort is made to keep prices low, it is sometimes necessary to increase prices at short notice. Wyndham Books reserve the right to show new retail prices on covers which may differ from those advertised in the text or elsewhere.

Postage and Packing Rate
U.K.
One book 25p plus 10p per copy for each additional book ordered to a maximum charge of £1.05

B.F.P.O. and Eire
One book 25p plus 10p per copy for the next 8 books and thereafter 5p per book. Overseas 40p for the first book and 12p per copy for each additional book.